Undoubtedly by Design

A (Summer) Romance at Pemberley

Michelle D'Arcy

Jo Abbott

Md'A

To all of us readers and lovers of Jane Austen and Pride and Prejudice who always want more of Darcy and Elizabeth and are persuaded they always belong together.

Thank you to all who contributed and helped in bringing this story into the light.

Thank you Lory for your nudges, Jo for the patience and explanations.

Thank you Marie, Christine-Elizabeth, Francesca, and Mihaela for your insight, remarkable suggestions, and kind encouragement.

And thank you to my most patient, steadiest fan, my husband.

To Pemberley, therefore, they were to go.

Jane Austen, Pride and Prejudice, ch 42

Prologue

Derbyshire, July 28th

She put the letter — a slip of paper holding the power to change so many lives — back on the table and glanced towards the window against which Darcy leant. She watched his uncharacteristically defeated posture and slumped shoulders for several minutes, not wanting to interrupt his thoughts, until he eventually turned away from the window, looking expectant, waiting for her impressions. For a long moment, Darcy and Elizabeth simply stared at each other, both too astonished to utter a single word, the letter lying open on the table, a sudden barrier between them.

The light-hearted delight and joy that had brightened their morning had swiftly turned into confusion and incredulity, the exhilaration into anger and guilt, just like dark clouds had suddenly covered the sun. She found the fortitude to break the heavy silence — but what could be said when so much was felt? What use might there be for words when feelings were so strong?

"I cannot fathom it... I know what we read, I understand the words, yet some of them I cannot comprehend..." Elizabeth finally whispered. "How is it possible? How could one dare...?"

"I...I would have never expected this..." Darcy swallowed thickly and continued more resolutely, "It is my fault alone. I allowed it to happen. I should have taken measures long ago."

"No, you cannot blame yourself, Mr Darcy. No more than I blame myself for my poor judgment and ridiculous misplaced trust," Elizabeth replied, fighting tears of shame and helplessness.

"I can and I do, Miss Bennet. I am to blame for this and much more. If only..." He hit his fist on the table, and the sound was as frightening as his dark countenance. Elizabeth startled and gasped, taking a step back.

He noticed and immediately turned to her, his voice changing utterly. "Forgive me, I did not mean to scare you. I shall find a way to remedy my wrongs, I promise. I will find a way to resolve it. That, I may promise you and myself," he vowed.

"I am not scared, and I trust you will do everything that is possible and beyond. Yet before that, sir, if I may..."

Chapter 1

Pemberley, July 25th — three days prior

T he abundance of candles and carefully placed mirrors made Pemberley's drawing room bright and sparkling.

The conversation carried on, interesting and amiable, and, as if from afar, Elizabeth recognised her aunt and uncle's animated voices. And *his* voice — calm, deep, composed, with a trace of a smile in it. The same little smile — barely there, not quite perceptible, but so meaningful — that he had worn from the moment he had happened upon her visiting his home and had greeted her with unexpected kindness.

By the time Elizabeth finally started the journey towards Derbyshire with the Gardiners, her usual joy and excitement for travelling had diminished proportionally with the growing tumult in her heart, and she struggled to conceal it from everyone around her.

Everything that had happened in the past months — Darcy's proposal, her rejection, his letter, the revelation of Wickham's true character and of her own foolishness and obstinacy — blended into a whirlwind of feelings and thoughts that had troubled her for months. Added to all this was her brief confrontation with Wickham after her return from Kent; the regiment moving to Brighton, and Lydia's incessant and loud whining and bragging about the colonel's wife's invitation to join her as her special friend; Jane's quiet but constant suffering; and her mother's endless complaints about Elizabeth refusing Mr Collins's offer and Charlotte Lucas accepting it.

When the Gardiners invited her on a tour to the Lakes, she accepted with gratitude and relief, hoping a long journey would settle her mind and heart. But the shortened trip they eventually settled upon only stirred her tumult.

Yes, Derbyshire was a large county. One would think she could visit it with impunity and without fearing an encounter. But three days ago, they had arrived in Lambton to visit Mrs Gardiner's relatives. Her aunt and uncle wished to tour the greatest house in the vicinity of the small market town, as they had done many others on their journey, and despite her awkward attempts to dissuade them, they had gone to Pemberley, with much reluctance from Elizabeth's side, and only after they had enquired and been assured that the master was not at home.

And yet, he had returned a day earlier than planned, just in time to find her wandering around his estate, enchanted by the beauties of Pemberley. If his marriage proposal had been the most unexpected and least imagined thing in the whole wide world, the meeting at Pemberley certainly counted as the most bewildering and mortifying encounter.

Her astonishment increased when, instead of treating her like his worst — or maybe, upon consideration of Mr Wickham, *second* worst — enemy and throwing her from his property, he behaved with perfect courtesy; in fact with a warm good-naturedness that stunned her. He was welcoming to her and amiable with her relatives. He introduced them to his sister's acquaintance and later invited Mr Gardiner to engage in gentlemanly activities with him, Mr Bingley, and Mr Hurst.

But even more amazing than his improved behaviour and charming manners was, to Elizabeth, her own reaction to him, the disconcerting sensations aroused inside her by simply being in his presence, and the frightening amount of time she spent simply thinking of him — which she had to admit that she had done a lot lately.

She was too ashamed of her past misjudgment and offensive rejection, too confused by the novelty of the changes in his demeanour and in her feelings to even attempt to analyse in depth what was happening. It was all too sudden, too soon, and too much for any estimation; and the fear of being mistaken yet again discouraged her even more.

Being invited to dinner at Pemberley was something the Gardiners, and even less Elizabeth, could not have imagined several days prior, and whilst all three of them felt honoured and delighted, they could not be completely at ease. Of the three of them, Mr Gardiner was the most comfortable, since he had already enjoyed the gentlemen's company on a fishing party.

The sharp sound of a high note — struck exquisitely on the pianoforte by Miss Georgiana Darcy — startled Elizabeth, reminding her to turn the pages for the girl. She had already sung while Miss Darcy played, but in truth, Elizabeth was well aware of how average her talent and musical proficiency were compared to the young miss, so she chose to assist and support her, rather than join her in performing.

From across the room, Elizabeth noticed Mr Bingley smiling with genuine pleasure, and she hoped he was thinking of Jane while looking at her. By his side were his sisters, whispering to each other with their usual self-sufficient expressions and apparent disapproval of her. Elizabeth was equally amused and annoyed by the two, as their barely concealed rudeness and contempt towards her were almost as laughable as their desperate attempts to flatter Mr Darcy and his sister.

When Miss Darcy had finished her performance and rose from the instrument, Louisa Hurst immediately took her place. Miss Darcy took a seat near her brother, and Elizabeth intended to sit opposite them, near her uncle and aunt.

Caroline Bingley's address stopped her though, and, although she expected the worst, the question still took her by surprise.

"Miss Bennet, has the militia regiment left Meryton?"

"Yes...they moved to Brighton for the summer," Elizabeth replied indifferently.

"I imagine it was a great loss for your family. I remember that you were particularly fond of one of the officers," Miss Bingley continued.

"I cannot imagine who you mean," Elizabeth answered, trying to keep her calm whilst noticing Darcy's sudden frown and pallor. Miss Bingley's attack was unmistakable, as well as her attempt to embarrass Elizabeth. But the effect of her statement was stronger and more painful for the Darcys.

"She means George Wickham," Mr Bingley interjected with genuine ignorance, trying to help Elizabeth. "Caroline, why would you bring up such a subject? You know Darcy cannot stand that man!"

The name, although mentioned with a good heart and the best of intentions, made Darcy clench his jaws and disturbed Georgiana so much that she seemed to cease breathing. She clutched her hands together in her lap and lowered her eyes, while Darcy tried to interject and stop the conversation.

"I certainly did not mean to offend Mr Darcy! I was only asking because I know how fond the entire Bennet family was of the regiment. Why, I still remember the Netherfield ball, when your younger sisters did little else the entire evening but entertain the officers. I wonder what they can be doing now, without that source of amusement."

The woman's tone was caustic and offensive, and Elizabeth fought the temptation to reply with all the bitterness and resentment she had gathered in the last months. Her genuine concern for the two Darcys tempered her ire, but she could not completely refrain from responding.

"We are handling the lack of amusement as best we can, Miss Bingley, as are the other residents of Meryton. The regiment is not as much missed as you imply. However, all our neighbours missed Mr Bingley last winter, and we all wondered about his sudden departure and his continuing to remain in London."

It was the Bingleys' turn to be surprised, and Mr Bingley mumbled something with embarrassment. Miss Bingley, however, replied with the same disdainful tone.

"When one is accustomed to superior society and life in London, it can hardly be expected to tarry in the country for too long. It is rather dull, especially in such a small, insignificant place."

"It was not dull to me, I assure you," Mr Bingley managed to reply. "In fact, I always said that the time spent at Netherfield was the happiest of my life."

"Oh Charles, you are too unsophisticated for your own good," Mrs Hurst said, rolling her eyes. "You should choose your company and your reasons for happiness much more carefully."

"This is nonsense," Mr Bingley responded with asperity and more determination than usual. "Happiness is a very personal matter. You cannot choose what and whose company makes you happy, it simply happens! The unrequited yearnings of your heart might make you unhappy, but disregarding them will not restore your happiness!"

"I believe you are correct," Miss Darcy timidly interjected, then immediately blushed as though she was surprised by her own statement.

"I am glad you are able to understand me and agree with me," Mr Bingley bowed to her. "I am certain there are things that Darcy cannot understand which make you happy, just like Louisa and Caroline cannot always understand my sources of happiness!"

"I heartily agree," Elizabeth said. "I cannot always understand or agree with what makes my sisters happy, but I wish nothing but the best for them, just as I am sure Mr Darcy wishes the best for his sister."

Her statement was not only an approval of Mr Bingley and Miss Darcy's statements, and a little help offered to Darcy, but also an elegant barb to Miss Bingley and Mrs Hurst, implying that they did not want the best for their brother. And nobody in attendance was oblivious to her meaning, which angered the Bingley sisters even more.

"Wishing the best for a brother or sister does not mean allowing an infatuation to ruin their future or their family prospects! Young people easily fall in love and come to regret it sooner rather than later, but the consequences are often difficult to overcome and repair!" Miss Bingley declared.

A glance was enough for Elizabeth to observe that Miss Darcy was fighting an uneasiness she could hardly bear, while Darcy's expression turned hard and inscrutable as he impetuously stood up.

"I would rather have a drink stronger than tea," he declared. "May I interest you gentlemen in joining me in the study? There will likely be some cigars too, if you care for them. And I shall request a fresh pot of tea for the ladies as well."

"I must beg you to excuse me," Miss Darcy said shyly in a little, lost voice but standing up to show her determination. "I am sorry if it prevents the gentlemen from withdrawing, but I am a little tired, and I would rather retire now. Miss Bennet, Mrs Gardiner, Mr Gardiner, I hope to see you again tomorrow?"

"We would be delighted," Mrs Gardiner answered.

Without thinking about it, Elizabeth rose too and grasped the young girl's arm as she would her own sister.

"Miss Darcy, you look a little pale. Are you unwell? May I help you to your room?"

"Oh no, Miss Bennet. You are very kind, but that will not be necessary. I am not unwell, I only need to rest."

"Miss Eliza," Miss Bingley interjected again, "I understand Pemberley is different from anything you have seen so far, but surely you can imagine there are over thirty servants in the household. There are enough maids to escort dear Georgiana to her room, there is no need for you to take on their responsibilities."

The insolent remark was too much even for Elizabeth, and she was prepared to fight back when Darcy's cold voice intervened.

"It is a privilege for me and Georgiana to welcome Miss Bennet, as well as Mr and Mrs Gardiner, to Pemberley. And I am certain Miss Bennet offered to assist my sister with genuine intentions, because of her generous heart, regardless of the number of servants."

Elizabeth blushed at the praise, while Miss Bingley and Mrs Hurst became red faced from anger.

"I am grateful for your care and concern, Miss Bennet," Miss Darcy added to her brother's praise. "And thank you for playing and singing with me."

"I thank you for patiently bearing my lack of musical skills and accomplishments," Elizabeth teased her gently. "And for delighting us with your wonderful performance."

"In truth, there is nothing Miss Darcy does not excel at," Mr Bingley declared with warm enthusiasm. "From playing to science and to riding, she is perfectly accomplished!"

"You are too kind to me, Mr Bingley," the girl answered. "If I am accomplished in anything, it is only to my brother's credit, and I am very grateful to him."

"The only credit I can claim is to be fortunate enough to have you as my sister, dearest," Darcy said affectionately. "Please allow me to escort you to the door and ask for Mrs Annesley to join you," he whispered as they walked out of the room together.

The affection and bond between the Darcys were obvious and touching, but there was also a palpable tension that Elizabeth could easily understand. The shadow of the previous year's events in Ramsgate had clearly not dissipated yet, and the pain caused by the vicious scoundrel Wickham still seemed to grieve them.

"Will you stay in Derbyshire long, Mrs Gardiner?" Miss Bingley enquired.

"Our plans are not fixed," the lady responded. "It depends on how much we enjoy our time here."

The short answer displeased Mr Bingley's sisters and

satisfied Elizabeth. It was a little mischief from Mrs Gardiner, and a small act of revenge for the lack of civility she and Jane had been forced to endure from Miss Bingley and Mrs Hurst a few months ago in London when the arrogant and uncivil sisters had belatedly returned Jane's visit.

Irritated and resentful of Miss Bingley's incessant discourtesy, Elizabeth was tempted to mention Jane's presence in town, being certain Mr Bingley was still oblivious to it. But she restrained herself, fearing it might expose Mr Darcy to another unpleasant argument. His comfort, she realised, a bit surprised, was more important to her than retaliation.

The master of Pemberley returned a few moments later, in obvious ill spirits. His efforts to behave amiably were apparent, and he concentrated his attention upon the Gardiners and Elizabeth, purposely ignoring the Bingley sisters.

"Mrs Gardiner, Miss Bennet, I know Mr Gardiner will join us again for a fishing party tomorrow. If you wished to tour Pemberley Park, I would suggest and gladly provide you with a small phaeton. I am sure my sister will be happy to drive you."

"That would be wonderful, Mr Darcy! I mean, if it is not too much trouble," Mrs Gardiner replied, overwhelmed by such generosity. "I confess I have always dreamt of admiring the park in its entire splendour, and on foot it simply is not possible, even for such an accomplished walker as yourself, Lizzy. Dearest, I promise you will be enchanted!"

"From the little I have already seen, I am sure the whole estate is beautiful. I look forward to enjoying the views," Elizabeth said, then blushed again, fearing her praises might be misunderstood.

"We have toured the park more often than I can remember, which is understandable since we visit Pemberley every year," Miss Bingley interjected again.

"That is precisely why I addressed the invitation only to Miss Bennet and Mrs Gardiner," Darcy replied sternly.

"Besides, neither you nor Louisa enjoy such rides," Mr Bingley added. "The last time we took a tour of the park, you declared it dull and demanded to return to the house rather quickly. But I know Miss Bennet is rather fond of outdoor activities. I still remember how she walked three miles from Longbourn to Netherfield, only to enquire after her sister. It was brave and kind-hearted!"

"I do not deserve such praise," Elizabeth replied, her cheeks still crimson. "I acted just as any caring and affectionate sister would have done."

"I agree with Bingley, Miss Bennet," Darcy said, and their eyes locked briefly. "It was truly brave and kind-hearted on your part, as was your concern for my sister just now. And I hope you will enjoy Pemberley's grounds as much as those in Hertfordshire."

"I have no doubt that I will, Mr Darcy. And I look forward to it," Elizabeth replied, wondering that she had never noticed before how warm and tender his dark gaze could be.

An hour later, the visit ended, and the guests were offered a carriage to return to the inn in Lambton where they had taken rooms. There would have been more regrets on both parts if not for the certainty that they would meet again the following day.

Darcy helped the ladies into the carriage, his eyes, as well as his fingers, meeting Elizabeth's again. His heart was full, pounding stronger than ever before, and he stared after the party until they disappeared from his sight.

Only then did he return to the house, just in time to hear the Bingley sisters abusing Elizabeth while Hurst was filling his glass once more.

He was in no disposition to bear such company, so he ended any conversation with a simple request.

"Bingley, before we retire for the night, I need to speak to you briefly. There is something that I must tell you regarding Miss Bennet. Miss Jane Bennet, who stayed in London throughout the spring."

Bingley stared at him, bewildered, while Caroline Bingley spilled her tea and Louisa Hurst gasped loudly.

Chapter 2

Darcy woke with more enthusiasm than he had felt in years. He prepared for the day, then went to the library.

The previous evening, having Elizabeth and her relations as guests in his house had been like a dream come true. A lasting dream that had been seemingly ruined at Hunsford by his disastrous proposal. And yet, he had been fortunate enough to be given a second chance. A chance to prove himself to Elizabeth, to show her he had taken her reproofs to heart and was able and willing to make amends.

One major step forward was to confess to Bingley his error in judging Jane Bennet's feelings, as well as his own role in concealing the lady's presence in town.

Although he had no occasion to base his confession on his own recent observation, Darcy did not doubt Elizabeth's claim regarding Miss Jane Bennet's affection for Bingley. If there had been a scheme to induce Bingley to marry the lady to secure the Bennets' future, Elizabeth would not have refused his proposal. Or perhaps her hatred for him had been so strong that it had overcome even her concern for her family. Either way, Bingley was entitled to know the full truth and to act according to his own wishes and desires.

His friend's reaction had been less bitter and resentful than Darcy felt he deserved. Bingley's kind heart was so enlivened by his renewed hopes that he forgot any upset, and instead of being angry, he was thankful that Darcy had been in error about Jane Bennet's indifference and that, even though he had been mistaken, his friend had had his best interests at heart. It had been a humbling moment for Darcy.

"Brother, may I come in? Are you busy?"

Georgiana's sweet, timid voice interrupted Darcy's reflections, and he invited her in with a large gesture.

"You do not have to ask me, dearest. I am never too busy to forsake your company."

"Thank you — you are always too kind to me. I am sorry I left so suddenly last night. I hope I did not offend our guests."

"Not at all, I assure you. I am sorry Miss Bingley was such an annoyance. I noticed you were disquieted by her words, but she intended to make Miss Bennet uncomfortable."

"Miss Bingley's manners and deportment are different from what I remember. I believe...I fear she dislikes Miss Bennet."

"Yes, she does. And I must say, her pretension and impoliteness brought me to the edge of my patience. My own civility is wearing thin. I am struggling to remain composed for Bingley's sake."

"Miss Bennet does not seem too affected, though," Georgiana remarked.

Darcy smiled, mostly to himself. "No, Miss Bennet is not

so easily affected by any perceived rudeness. She possesses equal fortitude and self-confidence to retaliate against such attacks."

"Yes, she does seem to." Georgiana took a few steps to the window in silence, then spoke again.

"Was George a friend of Miss Bennet? You told me he was camped in Meryton, but Miss Bingley suggested they were close friends."

Darcy frowned at the subject and struggled to reply with more nonchalance than he truly felt.

"Yes, he was. As usual, he made friends quickly and easily. But also as usual, I doubt he was capable of keeping them too long."

"Papa said there were very few people friendlier and with an easier disposition than George," Georgiana said timidly, blushing at her audacity to contradict her brother.

Darcy's heart ached as he fought the temptation to reply that there were also very few as insolent, self-serving, and unscrupulous as Wickham.

But he refrained, as he could easily see that, even after the Ramsgate affair, Georgiana seemed to trust more the memories of their father's affection for Wickham and her own impressions of the kindness that scoundrel had showed her as a child than his own warnings.

She did not go through with her elopement with Wickham because of her sense of responsibility, her respect for Darcy as an older brother who was almost like a father to her, and likely from the apprehension and shame of how the scandal might affect their family. But she was still holding that reprobate in tender regard, confirming that, at least for the time being, to further reveal Wickham's real character would only grieve and confuse Georgiana more or even make her resent her own brother.

As he could observe from her reaction, Elizabeth did trust him and had accepted his explanation in the letter, opening her eyes to Wickham's deceptions without resenting him. But she was older, wiser, and very likely her own attachment to Wickham — if it ever existed — had not been as strong or as long in duration as Georgiana's. With his sister, he needed more patience, more care.

Or perhaps he was not a good enough brother to Georgiana and had failed to establish a real bond of trust with her. That might easily be the case, and the blame was entirely his.

"Dearest, I promise you that the moment I see Wickham seriously showing an interest in a profession and being determined to make an honourable living for himself, I shall help him in any way I can. I am still willing to fulfil our father's wish and support him, but I cannot agree to give him money which he would only waste on vices and cunning schemes."

"I feel you are too hard on him," Georgiana continued, this time turning pale. "He is not perfect like you, but very few people are, even our cousin says that."

"Georgiana, I am far from perfect. I am just trying to behave decently and to carry out my duties. You, Fitzwilliam, Bingley, and many of our other friends are doing the same. That is all I am asking of George Wickham. Am I wrong?"

The girl lowered her eyes. "No, you are not wrong. You never are. I was wrong to argue with you, and I apologise. I did not mean to sound disrespectful."

She turned to leave, but Darcy reached out and gently grasped her arm.

"My dear, please wait. I beg you never to apologise for expressing your opinions, even if they differ from mine. I desire your affection and trust, as well as your self-confidence, far more than your respect or, Heaven forbid, your fear of me! Never be afraid to speak your mind and act as your heart tells you. I wish nothing but the best for you. Your happiness means more to me than my own."

Georgiana nodded and he embraced her, then she rested her head on his shoulder for a moment.

"I dearly love you, Brother, please do not doubt that. You have my deepest affection and complete trust. Even when I feel differently from you, I know you are not wrong. I wish to be happy without ruining *your* happiness."

The emotions overwhelmed the girl, and she remained silent in her brother's embrace. He caressed her hair, relieved to be able to comfort her, then he suddenly changed his tone.

"Well, I hope today will make both of us happy. I am sure Miss Bennet and Mrs Gardiner will be most enjoyable company for you. Will you take Mrs Annesley too?"

Georgiana pulled back, trying to present a tentative smile.

"No, I believe the phaeton will perfectly suit the three of us. Mrs Annesley will remain at home. Besides, she has toured the park several times already."

"Then you will drive the phaeton?"

"I will. Miss Bennet and Mrs Gardiner will arrive together with Mr Gardiner after breakfast."

"I might accompany you for a while if you and the other ladies do not mind," Darcy declared. "Just to be certain your ride goes well...not that I do not trust you...and then I shall go fishing with Mr Gardiner, Bingley, and Hurst."

He could not conceal his embarrassment while he attempted to sound indifferent. Georgiana's smile widened slightly.

"I am sure your company would be as pleasant for Miss Bennet and Mrs Gardiner as it would be for me. What a fortunate coincidence that they happened to visit Pemberley just when we returned home. A week earlier and we would have missed them entirely."

"Yes, a very fortunate coincidence," Darcy agreed, more grateful than his words could express, or he would dare admit to his sister.

Their tête-à-tête was interrupted by Bingley, who entered rather impetuously after the most perfunctory of knocks. He apologised only when he saw Georgiana.

"Forgive me, I came to speak to Darcy...about today's schedule. Miss Bennet will come to Pemberley today, will she not?"

"Yes. Georgiana will take her and Mrs Gardiner for a ride about the park. We discussed it last night at dinner."

"Yes, yes, I remember. May I come with you?"

Georgiana looked at him, taken aback, then glanced at her brother.

"Where, Bingley?" Darcy enquired, equally confused.

"Wherever Miss Bennet goes. I wish to speak to her. I have been thinking about it all night, and I have decided I should like to return to Netherfield. I would like to open it again. I still hold the lease, as you know...but before that, I want to ask Miss Bennet if she approves of it. I mean...if the neighbours would approve of such a decision."

The more restless Bingley grew, the more he mumbled, and the clearer his intentions became to Darcy and Georgiana.

"Forgive me," the girl interjected. "I understand you have matters to discuss, so I shall leave you now. I must prepare for the ride."

Both men nodded, and as soon as Georgiana left the library, Bingley continued, "Darcy, you may not agree with my plan, but I am determined to follow it...unless Miss Bennet suggests otherwise!"

"Bingley, I certainly do not disagree, and I applaud your determination in following your wishes, regardless of my or others' opinions."

"You do? I am glad to hear that!" Bingley replied hastily.

"However, if you will allow me to make a suggestion, perhaps following Miss Bennet on this ride — she in the phaeton, with Georgiana and Mrs Gardiner near, and you alongside on horseback — would not provide you with the right opportunity to speak to her. What would you do? Chase after the phaeton, shouting to cover the horses' hoofs? I intend to invite her and her relatives to dinner again tomorrow evening. I shall arrange for you to sit near her, so you will have an appropriate setting and enough time for any conversation you wish."

Bingley's face brightened.

"Would you? Yes, yes, that is a wonderful idea. Much better, indeed. So, do you approve of me opening Netherfield again? I may write to my housekeeper immediately."

"I do not approve of your haste in making any decision, Bingley," Darcy smiled with more understanding than usual. "But I cannot fault your eagerness in remedying a wrong for which you are not guilty."

"I am guilty, Darcy! I cannot deny that your advice weighed heavily in my decision to leave Netherfield, and I cannot excuse my sisters for their deception. But, in the end, I am the most to blame. I should have trusted my feelings more, and I should have judged Miss Bennet more accurately based on my own impressions and observations. I should have been more the kind of man worthy of Miss Bennet's good opinion."

"Then allow me to share the blame with you, Bingley. I was not the kind of man worthy of Miss Bennet's good opinion either," Darcy admitted with a bitterness that Bingley mostly missed.

"Well then, it is all settled! Shall we have breakfast now? I am very hungry," Bingley said enthusiastically.

"Indeed we shall. I am quite hungry myself," Darcy answered. More than hungry though, he was both eager and nervous, impatiently counting the minutes until he might spot the Gardiners' carriage bringing Elizabeth back. Back to Pemberley. Back to him.

∞ ∞ ∞

Elizabeth breathed in the fresh air of Pemberley Park in the summer, intoxicated by the scent, by the beautiful and colourful view, and not less affected by the muddle of feelings and thoughts that tightened the knot in her stomach. She was going back to Pemberley, but this time by design, at the invitation of its master, with no doubts of their reception.

The Gardiners had been in wonder — and a bit suspicious at first, truth be admitted — of Mr Darcy's generosity and amiability, and speculated about the reason behind such behaviour. Eventually, they concluded there could be no other reason but a peculiar and long-standing admiration by the gentleman for their most deserving niece.

They attempted to question Elizabeth about the gentleman, but her answers were uncharacteristically subdued and hardly satisfying. In the end, they respected her reluctance and ceased the enquiry, determined to observe the couple with further careful attention. Regardless of the reason, the invitation to spend time at Pemberley flattered and honoured the Gardiners, and they decided to fully enjoy its benefits.

As the carriage passed the park gate, crossed into the stunning estate, and approached the house, Elizabeth's heart pounded, and breathing became more difficult.

She was thrilled but still apprehensive of the moment she would face Mr Darcy again.

His handsome countenance had invaded her sleep, and dreaming of him the entire night had allowed her little rest.

Her struggle to find another explanation for his friendly and courteous manners failed, and she reluctantly admitted — although only to herself — that his affections for her seemed unchanged and unfaltering. But was it possible? Could a man so horribly abused, rejected, and so deeply offended, forgive and forget — and consider renewing his proposal? Was that possible?

The notion, as improbable as it was, thrilled her more than anything else in her life previously, but prudence demanded her restraint and her thorough examination of the whole situation.

Was it possible that her own feelings could have suffered such a dramatic turn, that her wishes could have changed so utterly while he remained so loyal to his purpose? Was she so shallow while he was so steadfast? If so, was she even worthy of his ardent love — as he had called it himself?

Lost in her reflections, Elizabeth was startled when Mrs Gardiner called her name expectantly. Only then did she notice the carriage had stopped in front of Pemberley's Palladian portico, and her heartbeat rose again.

Mr Gardiner jumped down, eager to indulge himself in his favourite activities. As he hastily helped his wife out of the carriage, Mr Darcy himself suddenly appeared in Elizabeth's view.

She held her breath, staring at him, and it was not long before their eyes met and locked. Her uncle called to her impatiently, but she was oblivious to everything else, all her attention focused on Darcy. Eventually, he stopped near the carriage, greeted the Gardiners distractedly, and stretched out his hand to her.

"Miss Bennet…" he said, and his voice made her quiver.

"Mr Darcy…" she whispered, placing her hand in his strong palm while his fingers closed around it. When she stepped onto the ground, her knees betrayed her, and she almost fell, but his arms — strong but gentle — steadied her, offering both support and comfort.

"Welcome back to Pemberley, Miss Bennet. We are happy to have you again," he said, so close to her that she could feel his warm breath.

"Thank you, sir. I am happy to be back," she answered softly but sincerely.

"Allow me to escort you. My sister and Bingley are waiting for you," Darcy continued, offering his arm to Elizabeth.

She took it with tingling fingers, walking by his side, nervous but delighted. Darcy stopped for a moment, waiting for Mr and Mrs Gardiner, and Elizabeth found herself enraptured by the simple privilege of taking his arm and overjoyed for every moment she was spending near him. Furthermore, she would rather stay there, she realised, in front of the house, on his arm, instead of visiting the beauty of the Pemberley grounds without him.

"Miss Bennet, Mrs Gardiner, I hope you are ready for the ride?" Mr Darcy asked.

"We are, very much so! And we are very grateful to you and Miss Darcy for making it happen," Mrs Gardiner responded enthusiastically on behalf of them both, while Elizabeth slowly but reluctantly withdrew her hand from his arm.

She was ready for the ride, but not quite ready to leave his side — yet, she had to. But her heart eased slightly as she knew she would see him again soon.

Chapter 3

A groom brought the phaeton around, two Dartmoor ponies hitched to it, one black and one white, both stunningly beautiful.

Georgiana approached and greeted them, together with Mrs Annesley. She was dressed in a lovely ensemble, with a little blue hat that complemented her countenance and her eyes. She smiled at them warmly, although she seemed to still wear her usual reserve. Mrs Gardiner returned her greetings just as warmly and moved closer to Mrs Annesley, while just behind Georgiana, Mr Bingley appeared — his smile so bright, so large, spread over his entire face as to become instantly infectious.

"Mrs Gardiner," Mr Bingley bowed in greeting and approached Elizabeth almost bouncing. "Miss Bennet, I have come to wish you a pleasant day! And to tell you that I discussed it with Darcy last night, and I have decided to reopen Netherfield. But only if Miss Bennet approves of it...I mean, if she believes that my return would not upset the neighbours..."

Mr Bingley became anxious as he spoke, his cheeks

changed colour, and his smile dimmed visibly.

Mr Darcy rolled his eyes, annoyed by his friend's impetuosity. They had particularly discussed only this morning that he would not bring up that rather delicate subject until the next day at dinner, but Bingley was a stranger to such notions as patience and prudence. He looked at Elizabeth in alarm, but seeing her expression of delight at the news, he calmed.

"Mr Bingley, I assure you that opening Netherfield again would be exceedingly pleasant for the entire neighbourhood," Elizabeth replied, surprised by the impromptu enquiry. "Unless you choose to close it again soon, of course," she added meaningfully, and Mr Bingley paled with some panic.

"Oh no, that would not be the case, I assure you. I intend to remain at Netherfield for as l...for an undecided amount of time...but a long one!"

"That is lovely to hear," Elizabeth approved, glancing at Mr Darcy. He seemed slightly irritated, and she wondered with some worry whether he still opposed his friend's association with her sister. And how did Mr Bingley's sudden decision occur? Had Mr Darcy mentioned something to him? Was he aware of his friend and sisters' uncalled for intervention? Had he been told Jane had been in town for so many weeks?

"Yes...and...I must apologise. I confess that I was not informed about Miss Bennet...the eldest Miss Bennet...Miss Jane Bennet being in London this past winter and spring. Darcy only told me last night. Had I but known, I would have certainly called on her and your uncle and aunt. I must apologise to her... to all three of them...I hope they will forgive my foolishness... I was uninformed," Mr Bingley spoke barely coherently, his discourse a mere babbling by the end.

"I dare assure you they will forgive you. Having your

company, belated as it may be, would be fine compensation for the past," Elizabeth said, taking pity on him and attempting to comfort him with another friendly smile. Her doubts had been answered. Mr Darcy had revealed the truth and very likely supported Mr Bingley's plans regarding Netherfield. She felt Mr Darcy's stare upon her and looked up to meet his eyes briefly, then turned her attention back to Mr Bingley.

"I shall leave you now to your ride. We shall speak more of this tomorrow evening," the young gentleman announced. "Darcy has told me you will all dine at Pemberley. I would have come with you now, but Darcy said I would be better not to bother you. I believe he is right, but I am glad I asked you, Miss Bennet. I shall write to Mrs Nicholls right away!" Mr Bingley finished this subsequent bout of babbling with an intonation that made it sound more like a question than a statement.

Elizabeth could not conceal her amusement, and she looked again at Darcy.

"You need my approval to write to your housekeeper, Mr Bingley?" she teased him.

Mr Bingley panicked again. "No, not at all. But I should like to know I have it, nevertheless. I mean...I look forward to returning to Netherfield, but I do not wish to upset anybody with my presence..."

Elizabeth was very tempted to reply that the only ones who may be upset would be his sisters, but she restrained her impulse to be impertinent.

"Mr Bingley, I am absolutely certain that your presence would please *all* your friends and neighbours in Hertfordshire. As I already said, you have been dearly missed."

"Excellent! I have missed them too...excellent!" he carried

on, then moved closer to the other ladies, where Mrs Gardiner was talking animatedly about her visit to Lambton with Mrs Annesley and Georgiana.

Darcy took one more step towards Elizabeth, and she tried to offer him a smile, although his nearness pleased and discomfited her at the same time.

"I hope you approve of Mr Bingley's decision too, Mr Darcy."

"To write to his housekeeper?" he teased her gently, then he grew serious again. "I do, but that is of little importance. I confessed to him all the details I knew concerning your sister."

"Thank you, sir."

"Please do not thank me, Miss Bennet. I am already ashamed of myself, knowing that my misgivings might have ruined my friend's chances of happiness. I only hope my confession has not come too late."

"I dare say that your confession was well timed, sir. And while you know how much I disapproved of your past intervention in this matter, having done it with your friend's best interest in mind should compensate for the guilt you feel."

"You are too generous with me. Bingley is a good man — and he is happier about returning to Netherfield than he ever was angry for being advised to leave it."

"He is a good man, indeed. And so is a friend who, although he gave him a wrong opinion in the past, tries to correct his error and advise him better in the present," Elizabeth said genuinely.

"I am doing my best, which often is not enough," Darcy

said, and Elizabeth sensed there was more behind his words. "I insisted that Bingley decide for himself, without haste and without asking for anyone's opinion or approval. Of course, he listened but disregarded my suggestion completely, as you just witnessed. But perhaps it is for the best. The suggestions I have given him in the last year have been rather poor."

"I am sure not all your suggestions have been poor," Elizabeth answered. "I understood you had something to say when it came to renting Netherfield, which was excellent advice."

Her voice sounded more flirtatious than she intended, and she lowered her eyes with embarrassment, failing to notice his pleasure at being the target of her liveliness again.

"Netherfield is a fine estate with a fine prospect. It was an easy and reasonable choice," Darcy declared. "Speaking of Netherfield, do you have news from your family? Have you decided how long you will remain in Derbyshire?"

"Oh, I do not know yet. Our stay depends entirely on my uncle and aunt, I am at their disposal," she confessed.

"If so, I must find a way to charm Mr Gardiner and induce him to remain longer," Darcy said, and the meaning behind his words took Elizabeth by surprise.

"I believe my uncle is already charmed by Pemberley," Elizabeth managed to reply, trying to sound light.

"I hope you are too," he continued, their eyes locking one more time.

"Very much so," she admitted, and pleasure suffused his face again.

"And your family? At Longbourn?"

"Oh, yes...my family...they are all in good health. And all but one in good spirits." Seeing Darcy's expression, she quickly clarified lest he took it as a hidden reproach in regard to Jane again, "My youngest sister Lydia is not used to being denied. She is not pleased my father would not allow her to go to Brighton for the summer."

Darcy furrowed his brow, and with a voice heavy with disbelief asked, "Brighton? Where the regiment is camped?"

His question sounded admonishing, and it embarrassed Elizabeth even though he did not mean it to.

"She was invited by Colonel Forster's wife," she tried to explain. "I urged my father not to allow her to go, even when she begged him, and eventually she relented. Colonel Forster is a decent and trustworthy man, and he promised to watch over her, but I could not... Knowing... By chance, my father agreed with me that Lydia was too young to be by herself with so many distractions around."

"Of course, I understand. Whilst I certainly do not distrust the colonel, I cannot argue with your father's decision. I hope your sister will recover her good humour," he concluded politely. "I...if I may..."

"Yes, sir?"

"I wished to ask you something of a delicate nature..." He moved closer, leaning towards her, his nearness making her dizzy. What was he doing?

"Miss Bennet, my sister is not aware that I have told you about Ramsgate. She is still affected by the situation, and I fear she still holds tender memories of that scoundrel..."

"Please do not worry, sir. I shall not speak a word that might betray your trust and confidence or trouble Miss Darcy."

"Thank you, Miss Bennet. I have complete faith in you. I am truly pleased to see Georgiana interacting so easily with you and Mrs Gardiner. She is shy and usually reluctant with new acquaintances. Your company genuinely pleases her, and it is certainly a relief to me."

"We are honoured and delighted by Miss Darcy's company, I assure you, sir," Elizabeth declared with sincerity, and he acknowledged it with a small nod of his head.

"Lizzy, my dear, are you ready? Let us go!" Mrs Gardiner suddenly called to her. "Miss Darcy will drive the phaeton for us. This is such an honour and a delight!"

"Yes, I am ready," she answered, smiling when her aunt repeated word for word her appreciation of Miss Darcy. She approached the phaeton, finding the young girl already had the ribbons in her hand, and her aunt had already installed herself on the bench, bouncing with anticipation.

"Please allow me," Darcy offered his hand, helping her up. She accepted his help, the touch of his fingers burning her even through her gloves.

"I shall see you to the park gate," Darcy declared, mounting his stallion that the groom had been holding nearby. "Bingley, I shall join you shortly. Please take care of Mr Gardiner and Hurst," he shouted while the horses started to move at a hasty pace.

With the gentle summer breeze caressing her face, Elizabeth allowed herself to be spoilt by the beauties surrounding them, but the presence of Darcy on his horse was reason for equal entertainment and distraction for her. Pretending she was just admiring the view, she could not help throwing surreptitious glances at him, noticing the fine figure he cut while riding and wondering about his reason for joining them, hoping she knew it but still fearful to see too much in his actions.

Miss Darcy slowed the horses as they approached the gate, and Darcy did the same.

"I shall leave you now. I cannot neglect my other guests any longer," he smiled. "Georgiana, please ask Miss Bennet and Mrs Gardiner to stay for refreshments when you return to the house. I shall ask that everything be ready and waiting for you. And hopefully, we shall be there too."

"Very well, Brother. Do not fret so, all is well."

"I am not fretting, dearest. I trust you, as well as Mrs Gardiner and Miss Bennet. Enjoy your time, and we shall meet later."

He turned his horse, and Elizabeth could not help but look back at him, once again admiring his posture and steady seat. He turned his head, gave her a brief nod, and then sped his horse to a gallop.

The moment he disappeared from her sight, Elizabeth realised that Pemberley — as beautiful as it was — lost a lot of its charm in the absence of its master.

The tour of the extensive park lasted several hours, and Elizabeth delighted in the variety of the landscape, often letting gasps of admiration escape her lips as the property's greatness unfolded in front of their eyes. Miss Darcy offered them explanations, many of which, she admitted, came from her brother, who loved and respected their legacy, to which Mrs Gardiner added memories of her happy times spent in Lambton.

Elizabeth was mostly silent; what could she say to express her true feelings? She was still incredulous that he had offered to make her mistress of that whole place, all that beauty, now that she comprehended that to be mistress of Pemberley meant something! Overwhelmed by the responsibilities attached to the position of Mrs Darcy, she could not help but contemplate what extraordinary sources of happiness the future Mrs Darcy would also have.

Suddenly, a sharp grip of pain and jealousy reminded her that she had refused him, and he would likely find someone else who would happily agree to stand by his side, who would be more suited to the position, more appreciative of the honour of the affection he bestowed on her... Someone he would smile at, someone he would hold hands with, someone he would share all this beauty with, someone who would join him in long rides and walks across the estate, in complete privacy. Someone he might touch with ungloved hands, dance with closer than was proper, someone who would feel the warmth in his eyes, the joy of his smile, and enjoy the caresses of his gentle fingers, the touch of...

"Lizzy! Lizzy, my love, are you listening?" Mrs Gardiner's voice startled her, and she turned to her companions with a forced smile, struggling to conceal her mortifying thoughts.

"Yes! Please forgive me, I am completely enchanted, bewitched by your home, Miss Darcy, as never before."

"I perfectly understand you, Miss Bennet. I have seen it every year since I can remember, and I am still enchanted every time," the young girl answered.

"Lizzy, we were talking about Mr Wickham. I told Miss Darcy that I made his acquaintance at Christmas, at Longbourn, and that you used to be good friends but seem to have grown rather cold towards him lately."

Elizabeth tried to keep her composure and not betray her panic while searching for the proper words. What else had her aunt said to the girl that she had missed?

"Mr Wickham was a friend of our family, like several other officers from the regiment stationed in Meryton," Elizabeth eventually replied. "I met him last autumn, and we were in company — with him as well as with his fellow officers — several times. I do not know him well enough to judge his character accurately. I travelled to Kent last spring and shortly after my return, the regiment moved to Brighton, so he remained but an acquaintance."

"Well, since Mr Darcy and Mrs Reynolds seemed to disapprove of Mr Wickham, I would rather trust their judgment," Mrs Gardiner said, much to Elizabeth's distress.

"George is a good man in his heart. My father loved him very much, and he was my friend throughout my childhood," Miss Darcy said in a trembling voice, and Elizabeth noticed the girl's hands were shaking on the reins.

"I hope Mr Wickham is as good in his heart as he should be, to honour your father's memory and your affection, Miss Darcy," Elizabeth uttered. "Oh! Look how the sun falls on that grove! It looks like a pond of sunshine!" she exclaimed, desperately trying to change the subject.

"It is lovely," Miss Darcy admitted. "We could stop there, let the horses graze and stretch our legs," she suggested, and Elizabeth agreed with an enthusiasm that was slightly forced and not a little relieved.

After a delightful stroll between the trees in the sunshine, they made their way home. Miss Darcy was amiable and friendly with them, answering Mrs Gardiner's questions and sighs of admiration, but Elizabeth could feel that Darcy was right; the girl was still troubled and indeed harboured no hard feelings against Wickham. Yes, she might have confessed the scheme to Darcy herself, but it was her conscience and her inner good nature that had prevented her from grieving and offending her older brother and not the admission of a dishonourable proposition or action on Wickham's part.

Whilst Elizabeth had been angry at the revelation of Wickham's deceptions and offended by how he had treated her like a fool to get revenge against Darcy, and she still held a solid grudge and resentment against him, Georgiana Darcy seemed to resemble Jane and see only the good in people. Smiling to herself, Elizabeth mused that, if a certain desired event would take place, Jane and Miss Darcy would be in company rather often, and, based on similarity and affinity, they would surely be the best of friends. Those reflections quickly led Elizabeth's mind to others, realising that if Mr Bingley did eventually join their family, she would also be in Darcy's company rather often. She could not decide whether she hoped for or dreaded such circumstances more.

She had her answer late in the afternoon when they returned to Pemberley and Darcy came to welcome them, together with Mr Bingley and Mr Gardiner. And, while Darcy hurried to offer his hand like he feared he might lose the opportunity, Elizabeth placed her hand confidently in his palm. At that moment, she also had the final confirmation that indeed, Pemberley's beauty was magnified by the presence of its master.

Chapter 4

"**M**y coat," Darcy asked his valet so brusquely that the man who had served him for years could hardly disguise his raised brows.

"The brown one, sir?"

"No, the green one," Darcy requested irritably, and a moment later he felt embarrassed. He realised he was behaving like a schoolboy; poor Stevens was blameless, and surely the colour of his coat would not affect Elizabeth's opinion of him.

However, regardless of what the reason might have been, her opinion of him had changed and improved, lifting him from dark despair to bright hope within only a few days. Her coming to Pemberley was the answer to all his doubts and prayers, although he had abandoned most of them after that dreadful April day at the parsonage.

"Stevens, I shall be away from the house this morning. I have business to attend to in Lambton, and I am not sure how long it will last. Bingley and Hurst plan to go fishing again, but in case they need anything, I am counting on you to be of assistance in any matter. Mrs Reynolds will take care of the ladies."

"Of course, sir. You may rely on me at any time."

"Yes, I know." He glanced at his image in the mirror and, satisfied enough, said, "This will do."

Then, impatiently, he left his rooms and hurried downstairs, followed by the valet's disapproving gaze.

In the main hall, Darcy was met and greeted by the housekeeper, Mrs Reynolds, who was instructing two of the upper housemaids and a footman. When they spotted the master, and after curtseying and bowing respectively, the three servants disappeared from sight to carry out their assignments.

"Mr Darcy, do you have any particular requirements for dinner tonight?" Mrs Reynolds enquired.

"No, nothing particular. I expect everything to be perfect, but I trust that will happen, as always."

"Of course, sir."

"Is breakfast laid out already? I am in somewhat of a hurry."

"Almost, sir. It should not be longer than a few minutes."

"Good. Have you happened to see Georgiana today?"

"She has not come down yet, sir. Nor have your guests."

"Please inform my sister that I shall be in the library, and I would like a word with her before breakfast."

"Certainly. I shall send word at once."

Darcy continued down the hall to his favourite and most used room in the house. In the comfort of his familiar spot, amongst his beloved books, he recollected the Netherfield library and the day when he had spent half an hour alone with Elizabeth, both reading.

It was the time when his infatuation with her had begun, and he had been arrogant enough to assume she was not only aware but anticipating and welcoming his attentions. Consequently, he tried to disguise his admiration by remaining silent and aloof. Thinking he had paid her too much attention during those first evenings at Netherfield, he had proceeded to avoid her or squarely ignore her, like he had done in the library. He had almost congratulated himself on his charity, not willing to give her false hopes in his regard! What a ridiculous, pompous fool he had been! He needed a horrible marriage proposal and a dreadful rejection to understand she was not just ignorant of his sentiments, but that he had to fight and struggle more for the privilege of pleasing and bestowing admiration and affection on a worthy woman.

"Brother?"

Georgiana's little voice drew him out of his thoughts and caught his attention as she entered reluctantly. She was already dressed for the day, but she was pale and seemingly tired.

"My dear, are you feeling ill? You look exhausted!" he said, stepping closer to her.

"I am well, please do not worry," she whispered. "I have not slept well, that is all."

"I am afraid all this agitation is too much for you. You should remain in your room and rest."

"Oh, no, that is not necessary. Quite the opposite, I think some time outdoors would help me."

He gently took her arm and directed her to a sofa, where they sat together.

"Then will you join me in Lambton? I have business to attend to, but you may call on Miss Bennet and Mrs Gardiner in the meantime. I plan to stop and greet them anyway."

"Oh, I would like that, but I must visit the Skinners again. Mrs Reynolds has prepared a large basket with food and fruit for the children, since Mrs Skinner is still too ill to even cook. She has also prepared them sheets, blankets, linen, and clean clothes. Mrs Reynolds has taken care of everything."

"Then I should come with you and go to Lambton later."

"Oh no, no! There is no need to alter your schedule, Brother. Mrs Annesley and a maid will accompany me. They will take the carriage because there is a lot to be carried. And I shall ride. I…you can trust me."

"I do trust you, Georgiana, you must stop worrying about that. Do you think the children would be better attended to if we brought them to Pemberley until their parents feel better? There are enough rooms in the servants' wing and enough maids to take care of them. It might be easier for the Skinners and safer for the children."

"That is so generous of you, Brother! Yes, it might be for the best! I shall speak to Mrs Reynolds, and she will ask the doctor about the Skinners' present condition. But…I think we must request their parents' approval for such action," she added timidly.

"Of course. But dearest, are you sure that the Skinners' illness is not contagious? I would not want you to be in any danger. Perhaps I should go with you after all."

"Brother, you have already asked Dr Hammond about them several times. He insisted it was from the bad mushrooms they ate, nothing more! He is confident they will get better soon, but they will likely feel the aftereffects for a while. To be honest, it is a miracle they survived and even more so that they did not feed them to the children too."

"That was so foolish and irresponsible of Skinner! As soon as he is better, I shall have another word with him! What was he thinking that he did not ask for my support if his food supplies were short?"

"You already spoke to him, Brother, and he told you he did not want to bother you and beg for charity. He said you had already helped him enough. He was just waiting for the harvest and thought they would pass the summer months with what they had and what they could find on the grounds. He is a hardworking, proud man, Brother. You cannot fault him for that."

"I do not fault him, but I regret that he did not trust me enough, that his worry for his family was not stronger than his pride. Though I do know the feeling of allowing yourself to be guided by pride," Darcy responded. "Most of the time, it leads to bad consequences. Hopefully, the Skinners' suffering will end soon."

"I shall inform you of what Dr Hammond says," Georgiana assured him.

"I might call on the doctor myself when I am in Lambton. And I might stop to visit the Skinners after all on my way back.

But Georgiana, are you certain you feel well?"

"Very much so, Brother. You should really not worry about me. I have so many people around to take care of me."

"I know, dearest. But I do worry about you and always will. And, no, Georgiana, it is not because I do not trust you! I worry because I care about you." He smiled a little to reassure her. "If Miss Bingley and Mrs Hurst become too tiresome, you may politely withdraw from their company. I wish you to do what pleases you, not only what you feel is your duty."

"Thank you! I shall keep that in mind. It does please me talking to Miss Bennet and Mrs Gardiner," she said with a shy little smile. "Richard spoke highly of Miss Bennet when you returned from Kent, and now I see why. She is so kind and unassuming and clever."

"I am glad to hear your good opinion. I know they hold you in high regard too."

"I believe they enjoy your company as well, Brother," the girl replied meaningfully. "I heard Miss Bingley saying that you disapproved of Miss Elizabeth Bennet when you first met. That you despised her company and you argued with her all the time. Clearly that cannot be true!"

"Sadly, a lot of it is quite true, my dear. In fact, I grossly offended Miss Bennet when I first met her at an assembly. I called her tolerable and refused to dance with her. And she overheard me..."

Georgiana looked at him, doubtful.

"You did! Why?"

"Why? I could probably summon better excuses like

Bingley pestering me to dance as he always does or because I was already annoyed at being obliged by common courtesy to my friend and host to dance with his sisters or my dislike of large assemblies... But the truth is that I was an arrogant fool and considered everyone in Hertfordshire unworthy of my attention and civility."

"Oh no, Brother! I cannot believe that!"

"You should believe it, my dear, because it is a truth that I am ashamed to admit. I spoke with sarcasm and derision about almost everyone I met while at Netherfield, including Miss Bennet's family. You should have heard how patronising I was judging Mr and Mrs Gardiner without even knowing them. In company, no less. It was not my finest moment, and while I can still probably be considered proud, I am not proud of myself. I did not despise Miss Bennet at all, and I enjoyed my lively exchanges with her, but I can see now how my behaviour could have been perceived. I cannot blame *Miss Bennet* for despising *me*."

"This I really cannot believe! She certainly does not despise you, anyone can see it!"

Darcy smiled bitterly at his sister's heartfelt support.

"Mayhap she does not, not now...but we had a dreadful argument in Kent, and she clearly expressed her opinion of me. Her accusations were as painful as they were just!"

"But then...if I may ask, why did she come to Pemberley, if you were not friends?"

"She came purely by accident, as Mrs Gardiner already explained. And Miss Bennet insisted that she only agreed with her aunt's suggestion to visit Pemberley because she was specifically given assurance that we were not at home."

"Miss Bingley said that Miss Bennet came on purpose…"

Darcy rolled his eyes, annoyed.

"Caroline Bingley speaks so much nonsense that one cannot address it all. But I have no right to criticise her, as for a while I shared the same disapproval of the Bennet family. I even supported Miss Bingley's attempt to separate Bingley from Miss Jane Bennet."

"Dear brother, I am all astonishment! Now I start to wonder that you and Miss Bennet are so friendly to each other."

"Yes, I wonder too…" Darcy muttered mostly to himself. "Now if your good opinion of your older brother is not lost forever," he said with more enthusiasm than he felt, but managed to make Georgiana smile, "allow me to escort you — breakfast has surely been long ready. And I insist you promise me you will rest before dinner."

"I promise."

∞ ∞ ∞

The Bingleys and the Hursts were already gathered together, and based on their plates, had already started breakfast. They seemed to be in the middle of an animated conversation which ceased for a moment when Darcy entered.

"We were talking about fishing," Bingley said, after a

moment. "Do you think Mr Gardiner will join us again today? He is such a genial fellow, entertaining company, and quite proficient on any subject of conversation, from politics to sport and gossip."

"Awfully lucky at catching fish too," Mr Hurst added.

"For my part, I hoped we would have a peaceful and pleasant day among family, since tonight our party will widen anyway," Miss Bingley said.

"Yes, I too miss previous years when it was only us at Pemberley for the summer," Mrs Hurst added, as always in support of her sister.

"I confess I have found this year more animated and diverting. Do not mind me for saying so, as I mean no offence, Darcy, Miss Darcy, but as beautiful as Pemberley is, it has been a little too sedate and silent in the past," Bingley said.

"I do not mind, Bingley. In fact, I tend to agree with you. But Miss Bingley, Mrs Hurst, I trust your rooms are comfortable and pleasant and private enough to provide you with all the peace you might desire. I know I can count on Mrs Reynolds for that. Please do not feel obliged to join the rest of the party for any activity that you do not enjoy. You may also ask for your meals to be delivered to your rooms."

Darcy's reply was perfectly polite and showed the proper hospitality a host owed to his guests. Under his solicitous words however, his disguised rebuff was not lost on the Bingley sisters.

"My thoughts exactly," Bingley added. "You may do whatever you please, and so shall we! Besides, the Gardiners and Miss Bennet will leave soon. Until then, I intend to enjoy their company as much as I can."

"I did not mean that I wished to isolate myself in my room," Miss Bingley answered angrily. "But I cannot easily adjust to the notion of treating like family people that we all disapproved of until recently. But I am only a guest, so I have not much say in this. If I were to choose, I would rather listen to dear Miss Darcy playing the pianoforte the entire morning."

"How very kind of you to say so, Miss Bingley!" Georgiana interjected. "I thank you for the compliment, however, as much as I would like that, it will not be possible, as I need to visit some of our tenants. There has been an illness in the family, and they need supplies and possibly help. My brother even said we might bring the children to Pemberley until their parents are completely recovered."

Mrs Hurst almost choked and exchanged a quick look with her sister.

"My dear, your kindness is admirable, but is it safe? Maybe because you are still so young, you are enthusiastic, but is it not too much to visit the tenants so often, especially if they are ill and feverish? And bring the children here? Tenants' children at the house? What if they were to spread the disease?"

"I must support my sister," Miss Bingley uttered. "Would it not be enough to send some servants with the supplies? I never heard of an estate where both the master and his sister visited ill tenants every day. It does sound like an unnecessary endeavour."

"You may not have heard of it, but in truth, this is how the mistress of an estate should act," Darcy finally intervened in the exchange. "Or at the very least, the mistress of this estate. My mother behaved in the same manner, and I am very proud that my young sister is following in her footsteps."

Miss Bingley turned white, then red, blinked and

swallowed. "Yes, well...err...indeed, but what I mean—"

"Now, let us finish breakfast," Darcy interrupted. "I must go to Lambton. I trust you all will do what provides you comfort and entertainment while I am gone."

∞ ∞ ∞

When the maid announced Mr Darcy, the Gardiners and Elizabeth glanced at each other in wonder. They were invited to dinner that evening, which was already causing Elizabeth enough trepidation and restlessness to almost equal her uncle and aunt's pleasure and satisfaction. They certainly did not expect him to call, and for a moment, Elizabeth feared he might have changed his mind and come to withdraw the invitation.

There was not much time for speculation before he entered, bowing amiably.

"Mr Darcy! How delightful to see you! We did not expect to have the pleasure of seeing you until later in the afternoon," Mr Gardiner said.

"I had some business in Lambton and so took this opportunity to call on you. I hope I am not inconveniencing you." He stole only a brief look at Elizabeth, as short as the blink of an eye.

"Indeed not, sir, it is a pleasure," Mrs Gardiner declared. "We were just discussing our schedule. I promised to spend more time with my aunt and cousins since we shall soon have to return to London. I am trying to convince my husband to join me, but I am meeting with little success."

"In my defence," Mr Gardiner said, "as much as I respect your aunt and cousins, I have already exhausted all subjects of conversation in our previous visits. I believe my dull presence would mostly defeat the object of your meeting."

"You have become very spoilt, sir. Were you able to choose, you would spend the remainder of our time in Derbyshire catching fish at Pemberley," Mrs Gardiner scolded him playfully.

"I would not even attempt to deny it, my dear. It is an opportunity that came about in the most fortuitous way, and it might not occur again any time soon. So why not enjoy it to the fullest? Only my affection for you has restrained me from asking Mr Darcy's permission to sleep next to the stream," Mr Gardiner jested good-naturedly.

"If I may be allowed to interrupt," Darcy interjected with visible reluctance to disturb their familiar banter. "This is one of the reasons for my call this morning. I intended to invite you, if you do not have other previous engagements, to come to Pemberley earlier than planned and perhaps remain for the night to enable you to relax fully after dinner. I shall arrange for your trunks to be transported to Pemberley. And please do not mistake this as an arrogant boast, but I trust there are enough rooms at Pemberley so each of you can be provided with a most comfortable chamber. Mr Gardiner will not need to sleep next to the stream," he attempted to quip, which went mostly unnoticed due to the general astonishment provoked by this extraordinary invitation.

"That is, if it is possible and agreeable to you, of course... I would not wish to ruin your other plans..." he trailed off, hesitant, clearly uneasy at being faced with the stunned silence after voicing his proposal. He looked mostly at Mr Gardiner, but Elizabeth felt he truly addressed her. She was as astonished as the Gardiners by the invitation; she reasoned it might be meant for her and was grateful for the compliment, but she dared not imagine more.

"Mr Darcy, your generosity is beyond any expectation," Mr Gardiner said after a brief but meaningful glance at his wife. "I do not even know what to say...I mean...yes, we gladly accept your invitation, but I can hardly believe it. I should wonder as to the reason for it, but I dare say I can imagine it myself."

"This is a surprise, indeed," Mrs Gardiner added, visibly emotional. "Spending the night at Pemberley? This is...I never imagined that I..." Regaining her composure, she graciously acquiesced, "Certainly, we accept, sir, it would be an honour for anyone!"

All three of them turned to Elizabeth, who was still silenced by surprise. She knew her answer did not matter much to her uncle — who had already made the decision for them all — but it was of great importance to Darcy.

"I should like that very much," she whispered, and joy lit up Darcy's face instantly.

"Excellent!" he said. "Please let me know how you would like to proceed, which way is best for you..."

Mr Gardiner looked at his wife enquiringly, and she smiled at him, understanding what a favour she was actually granting him.

"Very well, Mr Gardiner. You and Lizzy may go now, so you do not waste another day of fishing. I shall prepare my trunk now but shall come with our carriage later on, as soon as I have completed the visit with my aunt."

If Mr Gardiner expressed his gladness openly, thanking his

wife and kissing her hands, Darcy and Elizabeth were no less eager and happy but expressed their rapture more cautiously. However, they had the time to lock eyes and share smiles that conveyed more than words could at that moment.

Less than half an hour passed until two small trunks filled with more than enough garments and finery for two days were packed.

"Mrs Gardiner, would it be agreeable to you if I sent my carriage with a coachman and a maid to convey you to Pemberley? That way, your coachman may remain to rest at the inn," Darcy offered further.

"That would be perfect, Mr Darcy," the lady readily agreed.

Elizabeth could not but admire his care and attentiveness, as well as his consideration for all the details that might affect the people around him. It was yet further proof of his remarkable character that she had so foolishly failed — or refused — to acknowledge for such a long time. And yet, he was there, offering his arm, ready and eager to take her back to his home and maybe — dare she hope it? — further into his life.

Chapter 5

In the small open carriage, Elizabeth sat in the middle, between her uncle and Darcy. The horses' gait and the unevenness of the ground made it impossible to remain still, and she tried to prevent herself from slipping and sliding by grasping the bench. While Mr Gardiner spoke to Darcy, Elizabeth's attention and all her senses were directed to the side where her body touched and brushed over Darcy's. Unlike her, he seemed unaffected by this closeness and preoccupied with the road ahead of them, occasionally answering Mr Gardiner's enquiries. However, Elizabeth could feel the looks he cast towards her from the corner of his eye.

She wondered if he truly had business in Lambton or had come only for them. For her. Was it possible? But if not, why would he take the carriage and not come on horseback? He did admit it was *one* of the reasons for calling on them: to invite them to Pemberley for an entire day and night. But what was the other reason? He had not mentioned it, so perhaps it was not important. Or perhaps he would reveal it later.

They arrived at Pemberley relatively quickly, and Mr

Gardiner expressed his impatience to join the other two gentlemen.

"We might check if they are already at the stream," Darcy suggested. "When I left earlier, they were already speaking of being prepared to go fishing."

"Yes, we might do just that," Mr Gardiner agreed. "If they are there, I shall join them. You do not mind, do you, Lizzy? I am sure you will entertain yourself with Miss Darcy and Mr Bingley's sisters."

"I do not mind, Uncle, how could I?" she teased him.

"I am not certain whether my sister has returned yet," Darcy explained. "She planned to visit some tenants this morning — I believe I mentioned to you the family that had been taken ill? They have three small children. Georgiana is very thoughtful and provides for them."

"Miss Darcy is very kind and generous," Mr Gardiner said. "Not many young ladies in her position would take so much trouble."

"Yes, she is. I believe kindness and generosity are her finest accomplishments, after all," Darcy admitted with much emotion in his voice.

They did not have to wonder for much longer about the two other gentlemen, as they could easily be spotted sitting by the stream, in the shadow of an old tree, with their fishing rods next to them, a bottle not far away and glasses in their hands. At seeing the carriage, they immediately waved joyfully. The first thing Elizabeth noticed was how different — more cheerful and easy-mannered — Mr Hurst was in the absence of his wife and sister.

Mr Gardiner climbed down from the carriage and was warmly welcomed.

"Darcy, will you come and join us?" Mr Bingley joyfully enquired.

"I might, later on. But carry on without me. I shall take Miss Bennet to the house first, then I have several more tasks to complete. I also need to speak to Georgiana and Mrs Reynolds as soon as they return from the Skinners'."

"I think they have already returned!" Mr Bingley answered. "We spotted the carriage — I believe Mrs Reynolds and Mrs Annesley were inside. Miss Darcy was on horseback, but I think she wished to take a longer ride because she turned away and entered the grove."

"Yes, Miss Darcy definitely did not ride towards the stables," Mr Hurst confirmed.

"Did she not? That is quite strange," Darcy replied, frowning. "She might have forgotten something, or perhaps she simply went for a longer ride to relax. I am sure we shall meet her if we drive through the park."

"Or perhaps she wished to delay returning home early, without you," Mr Bingley muttered sheepishly, sipping from his drink. "I cannot blame her, since my sisters can be rather trying at times."

"I second that," Mr Hurst interjected, raising his own glass. "I would choose to take a long ride myself were I not too lazy for such an activity. Thank God brandy always relaxes me instead."

Elizabeth stared at them curiously, barely concealing her amusement. She had never heard Mr Bingley speaking in such a manner about his sisters, and Mr Hurst even less. In truth, Elizabeth wondered whether Mr Hurst had spoken more than ten words in her company since they had become acquainted almost a year ago, and that included him asking her opinion about the ragout at Netherfield.

Eventually, Darcy bade his friends farewell and, holding the reins, gently but firmly nudged the horses onwards. Elizabeth felt a thrill down her spine as she realised she would be alone with him in the relatively small carriage, close to each other, although not necessarily touching as there was more space on the bench now. Darcy seemed composed enough, but he was silent, not desirous to start a conversation and seeming to scrutinise the grounds intently.

"Are you worried about Miss Darcy?" Elizabeth asked.

"Not about her — this is her home, there is no danger to her at Pemberley. There are plenty of people working all over the estate, and she knows every rock and every tree. Even her horse knows how to return to the stables by himself."

"Yes, I imagined as much, but I noticed your frown and concentration, and I wondered…"

He turned to her, and their gazes met. "You are very perceptive, Miss Bennet. I am more concerned as to why she would turn and enter the grove. I hope the situation of the tenants she visited has not worsened, as it was rather delicate to begin with."

Elizabeth asked him more about the case, and he offered her further details.

"The Skinners have been our tenants since the day they married, ten years ago," Darcy explained. "They are hardworking, honest people, who have fallen on hard times lately. When they both fell ill, I invited them to stay at Pemberley during their recovery — there was plenty of space in the household wing. But they have too much pride to accept."

Elizabeth watched him as he spoke, listening to his words and observing the small changes in his expression that revealed his feelings.

"I find it admirable that you are so concerned with the well-being of your tenants, Mr Darcy. We have only a few servants at Longbourn — they are like part of the family — and even fewer tenants. But to have so many people that rely on you and to know and care for everyone requires great character and a deep sense of responsibility. And a big heart."

"You are very kind, but I do not feel I deserve any praise. I am simply doing things as I learnt from my father. I have added some of my own ideas to increase the benefits to everyone, but if Pemberley is a successful estate, its success is mostly due to the work of the tenants, and it should be shared with them. If people are unhappy, their lives will be affected, as will their work."

"It seems a simple philosophy, and yet I feel there is more to it than that," Elizabeth replied. "Oh, look, is that not Miss Darcy?" she pointed to a rider who was crossing the park at a gallop.

"Yes, it is her. It seems she just went for a longer ride, after all."

"What a beautiful posture she has! And what speed!" Elizabeth continued.

"She is truly an accomplished rider," Darcy agreed. "Well, now that we have seen her, we may return to the house. I am sure she will join us soon."

Elizabeth was tempted to reply but restrained herself.

"It is my turn to say that I noticed you refraining from saying something, Miss Bennet. Is there anything wrong?"

"No, no…I was just reminded of Mr Bingley and Mr Hurst's comments, and I must say I agree with them."

"Regarding Miss Bingley and Mrs Hurst? I hope they do not annoy you too much. I know they can be undeservedly haughty, even rude."

"They can, but I have always been more amused than irritated by their insolence and snobbish ways."

"Yes, I know," he smiled. "I remember how you put Miss Bingley in her place several times. It was a pleasure to watch."

"Ah, so you have amused yourself at our expense, Mr Darcy. That is not very gentlemanlike on your part," she teased him.

"I admit I have, and I accept the blame, Miss Bennet. I particularly recollect one evening at Netherfield when Miss Bingley invited you to take a refreshing stroll about the room."

"I remember that evening too. It was when that lady claimed you were intimate friends."

Darcy rolled his eyes. "Miss Bingley uses the word *intimate* too often and always incorrectly when she speaks of me. It amused me for a while, but not any longer."

"Well, at least you do not have to live with them for too long. Mr Bingley and Mr Hurst do not have a choice. I am sorry to say it, but I truly pity them."

"I do too. That is why I provide them all the means of entertainment at my disposal while they are at Pemberley," Darcy playfully added, and Elizabeth laughed.

He smiled too, looking straight ahead, and Elizabeth's eyes were arrested by his profile for a few moments.

He looked as handsome as ever, but so relaxed that his mere presence was comforting and entertaining to her. She was alone with him, and there was nothing more natural, more pleasant. He was everything a gentleman should be, and if his easy manners and friendliness were not as exuberant as Mr Bingley's, his amiability was certainly deeper and more meaningful.

"I have to confess there have been times I have shared the same opinion as Miss Bingley and Mrs Hurst," Darcy added in a suddenly changed, more subdued tone. He seemed genuinely remorseful, and Elizabeth, comprehending his implication, briefly touched his arm with her gloved hand.

"We all make mistakes, Mr Darcy, and occasionally share the same opinion as people who do not deserve our friendship or our approval," she said daringly. Then with a deep breath, she continued, "Sometimes, the wrong might be remedied. At other times, it causes irreversible damage for a lifetime."

Her words affected both of them and heightened their mutual sense of guilt, plunging them into their own thoughts, the lapse in conversation causing a silence broken only by the sound of the horses' hoofs and the wheels of the carriage.

"True," he spoke at last. "Some of us are stubborn and arrogant enough to need a painful awakening before admitting the error."

"I hope that statement is meant for both of us, Mr Darcy, as

I recognise myself in it. I needed a long letter to open my eyes to the truth."

He gazed at her, and the tension suddenly increased between them, dimming the brightness of a most beautiful day. The feeling that she owed him apologies and explanations became even more overwhelming. She breathed deeply, gathering her courage. She had to speak her mind, and it might be the only opportunity for a private discussion.

"Mr Darcy, I beg your forgiveness for bringing up a most disturbing matter. But I can go no longer without thanking you for your generosity and amiability, which I know is much more than I deserve. I must apologise, although I know my past words cannot be either forgotten or forgiven. I know I do not deserve to be welcomed at Pemberley, and I am very sorry if my presence has troubled your serenity. My gratitude for your kindness towards my uncle, my aunt, and myself is beyond words."

She spoke with her eyes lowered, ignoring the beauty around her and trying to disguise the tears of shame that were moistening her eyes.

"Miss Bennet," she heard his voice interrupting her mortifying tirade. He paused, so she turned her eyes up to him, meeting his stare, which was darkened by the intent to dispel any misunderstanding.

"Miss Bennet, please know that no other guest has ever been more warmly welcomed at Pemberley, and nobody's presence has brought me more pleasure."

His admission stunned her almost as much as his declaration of love at Hunsford had, and she met it with almost as much doubt. But, unlike that dreadful day, she found no strength and no words to respond or argue except a shy, "Thank you."

"It is I who does not deserve the bestowal of your presence, and I beg your forgiveness for my prideful and arrogant past behaviour. The way I expressed myself through words and actions was appalling and deserves no excuse."

"You are too severe on yourself, Mr Darcy, and much too generous with me. If you were wrong, so was I, and if you acted with pride and arrogance, I acted with spite and prejudice. Neither of us is flawless, and apologies are required on both sides."

"Shall we argue for who bears the largest share of the blame, Miss Bennet?"

"No, sir. But I shall not allow you to take most of the fault upon yourself. Besides, you have already remedied most of your errors by confessing the truth to Mr Bingley and in your generosity towards my uncle and aunt."

"You too showed generosity and kindness to my sister, Georgiana."

"Perhaps, but it is not the same thing! Miss Darcy is a wonderful young lady, and her company is a delight. And we happened upon her, we disturbed her and you, we were the intruders. So we at least had to behave well enough to compensate for the favour you have granted us."

"So, you have been kind to my sister because I have been kind to your uncle and aunt?" he enquired half mocking, with a little bitter smile.

"Oh no, that is not what I meant! I admire her, and I like her very much. She is truly admirable, and anyone would be delighted and honoured by her company!"

"I could say the same about the Gardiners, whom I offended with my attitude long before I even met them. Fortunately, we both have fine relatives whose company we enjoy and who do not resemble us in flaws."

There was a trace of a smile in the corner of his mouth, and she tried to calm herself.

"Are you teasing me, Mr Darcy?"

"I believe I am, Miss Bennet. But teasing or not, I am being completely honest in my statements."

"I do not doubt you, sir. I already know that you abhor disguise of any sort."

The mere words brought back the recollections of that night at Hunsford, and awkward, painful silence wrapped them anew.

"I am very sorry," Elizabeth whispered, berating herself for the ill-timed and ill-worded quip. "I deeply apologise," she repeated.

"Miss Bennet, why do you repeat that? What are you sorry for? What are you apologising for?" he asked directly, catching her unprepared. She had no other option but to state the blunt truth.

"I am sorry for the unfair accusations and offences I threw at you. I am sorry for trusting Mr Wickham, like a complete fool blinded by prejudice. I am sorry for not being worthy of your trust and good opinion, believing his claims without the shadow of a doubt, like a simpleton," she admitted with emotion.

"Wickham has always been proficient in deceiving people. And he has been blessed with a pleasant figure and manners, with an appearance of goodness that helps him win friends quickly and the favour of ladies easily. There have been many others — men and women, and as you know even within my own family — who fell for his claims as readily as you did."

"Yes, but you see, sir, my stupidity was even greater, as I did not believe him because I was charmed by *him* but because I was prejudiced against *you*. I thought you despised me and my family and disapproved of my sister Jane enough to conspire with Mr Bingley's sisters against her. Therefore, I chose to believe the first person to support my ill opinion of you. And that day at Hunsford, I did not necessarily speak in his defence, but mostly against you."

His face was the image of remorse and grief, and she regretted starting the conversation that threatened to ruin her time at Pemberley.

"I must apologise further for bringing forth the remembrance of the past. Especially of that day at the parsonage. I am a very selfish and inconsiderate creature, indeed."

"It was not you who brought up the recollections, Miss Bennet. I have recalled that day only too often since last April. And every time I reproach myself for allowing it to happen. Were I not so arrogant, so wrong in my judgment, so presumptuous in my estimation, I would have never proposed that day and would not have forced you to listen to something that disgusted you so much and that you so harshly and rightfully rejected."

"I was equally wrong in my judgment and presumptuous in my estimation," she said. "And I am not certain whether I wish for the day to have never happened or not. But I know I regret most of what I said."

He stopped the carriage, lowered the reins, and turned to

better look at her. His gaze burned her face, and she lifted her eyes to look into his.

"You regret what you said that day?" he whispered. "You mean...?"

"I do not regret refusing you, Mr Darcy," Elizabeth hastened to make herself understood. "My feelings at that time were not of such a nature to justify an acceptance. Had I accepted your marriage proposal that day, I would have done it for the wrong reasons, and it would have been unfair to you. And now, after I have discovered your true character and your worthiness, I congratulate myself even more for having the strength to refuse a man like you. We were on unequal ground that day, not in regard to our situations in life but in our feelings. The rejection itself was proof of consideration for you and for myself. We, both of us, deserve better. The way I voiced my refusal and the reason that drove me to it were dreadful indeed, and that is what I regret."

He continued to stare at her from the short distance allowed by the carriage.

"I see...I never thought of it that way because I never expected a rejection, nor did I imagine it would be so hurtful. But now I am more convinced it was my fault alone. My behaviour led you to have an ill opinion of me and to trust Wickham. And the way I expressed myself during the proposal drove you to reject it and me the way you did."

"Mr Darcy, let us not argue about the share of blame again. Let us be grateful that we had the chance to speak openly and honestly. This conversation has been so valuable to me!"

"Yes...to me too...but, Miss Bennet, I noticed you spoke only about the past. Am I wrong?"

"You are not wrong, sir."

"Then…dare I assume your opinion has changed?"

"Very much, sir. Everything I felt and said that day remains in the past. The present is…more than I hoped and imagined a few months ago."

"I am very glad to hear that, Miss Bennet. Just as glad as I am of your presence at Pemberley. We are in complete agreement. This is much more than *I* hoped and imagined a few months ago."

He smiled, and her heart warmed while she replied, "I am delighted to be in complete agreement with you, Mr Darcy."

His smile widened, and he took her gloved hand, bringing it to his lips for a moment.

"We should continue our drive — Georgiana must be already home. But there is one more thing I must confess to you, Miss Bennet."

"What would that be, Mr Darcy?"

"I had no particular business in Lambton today…except visiting you and trying to convince you to come to Pemberley. I have been thinking of this little scheme since you left yesterday."

Her face coloured becomingly, and her smile matched his.

"I confess I suspected that, sir. In fact, I hoped it would be the case…"

"Good…good…now let us go home," he said, his words more meaningful than even he realised.

Minutes later, the carriage stopped in front of the main entrance. Miss Darcy was walking from the stables towards the house, and from a window on the upper floor, Miss Bingley and Mrs Hurst were glaring at them.

Chapter 6

With both Elizabeth and Georgiana at his sides, Darcy entered the house. He questioned his sister about the Skinners and was pleased to hear the doctor had recently examined them. He had reported that the danger had passed, and the parents would be fully recovered in less than a week. The children were under the supervision of the eldest girl, who was almost ten, and they refused to separate from their parents even for a short while.

"I am glad to hear such favourable reports, my dear. Miss Bennet and I were worried when we heard you did not return with Mrs Annesley and Mrs Reynolds."

"I did return but then went for a ride. I have a slight headache, and I thought some air and exercise would make it better."

"You are still pale," Darcy continued. "Perhaps I should call the doctor to examine you too."

"Please, no! Dear brother, you cannot bother the doctor for mere tiredness!"

"Then you should rest a little, I am sure Miss Bennet will not mind."

"No, not at all!" Elizabeth assured her. "And I must second Mr Darcy in this. You do look lovely as always, but pale."

"I shall be well after a little tea. And perhaps then we could take a stroll in the garden? Or anything you wish to do, Miss Bennet. I can postpone my pianoforte practice."

"In truth, I would be delighted to assist you in your practice. Hearing you perform is a pleasure I shall surely miss when I leave."

"Very well then," Georgiana answered. "I shall change my gown and return immediately."

"And I shall call a maid to show Miss Bennet her room," Darcy said.

"Is it in the east wing?"

"No, I thought the two rooms in the family wing would be more appropriate since the windows provide a full view of the lake and the park."

"Yes, it sounds a perfect choice," Georgiana agreed, while Elizabeth had to face another surprise. A flattering one, but certainly unexpected. While the Bingleys and the Hursts — friends of the master for a long time — stayed in the guest wing, albeit in their 'usual apartments', for her and her relatives, Darcy had prepared two of the family rooms. Could a gesture be more thoughtful and significant? Even if his reason was the declared one — offering them the best view — it was still exceedingly considerate and flattering. He had proved that he was constantly thinking of them and had made every effort to meet and exceed their expectations. Dare she assume he had done it for her? How could she *not*?

"Brother, I can show Miss Bennet her chamber, it is not far from my own. And she may ring for a maid if she needs assistance."

"Good! Excellent," Darcy said with visible contentment. "I shall be in the library if you need me." He knew he should return to the other gentlemen, but he purposely delayed leaving the house, hoping for more opportunities to interact with Elizabeth. Relieved that all was well with Georgiana, he rejoiced in reliving the brief yet significant conversation he had shared with Elizabeth in the carriage.

Her apologies, although he did not consider them necessary, proved that she had given much thought and consideration to that day which tormented her as much as it did him. She trusted his letter completely and accepted his explanations. The rejection had caused him tremendous pain, combined — for a while — with rage and resentment. The anger had been long gone before he returned to Pemberley, but the pain remained, strong and unsettling.

Her genuine admission that despite everything that had been cleared up between them, she did not regret her refusal and she did not wish to have accepted him for the wrong reasons touched his heart and induced him to admire her character even more. And the clear distinction she made between her past and present feelings offered him a lighter heart and a glimpse of hope that Elizabeth's visit to Pemberley and her stay in the family wing — and eventually perhaps in another room altogether — might last longer.

When Darcy eventually left his library in search of the other occupants of the house, finding all but Mrs Gardiner and the gentlemen in the drawing room, talking. Mrs Gardiner arrived and joined them, so Darcy thought better of intruding on the ladies and asked for his horse to join the gentlemen's party. However, before he could take his leave, his friends were returning — satisfied and boasting a little too loudly of their catch, and red-faced from the sun as well as from the wine they likely enjoyed a little too much.

The afternoon passed easily, with each spending time on their own preferences. Elizabeth listened to Georgiana practising her instrument, and then the two of them, along with Mrs Gardiner, took a long walk around Pemberley's park. Miss Bingley and Mrs Hurst declined such activity, claiming again they were already too well accustomed to Pemberley's beauty.

The gentlemen withdrew to the library, discussing politics, enjoying drinks, and making plans for returning to Hertfordshire, or in Mr Hurst's case, taking a nap on the sofa.

From time to time, Darcy reverted to his old habit of approaching the window, but now it was only to stare through it, watching the ladies stroll in the garden. The image of Elizabeth and Georgiana side by side, smiling and talking animatedly, was one that he wished deeply imprinted in his mind, so he could recollect it in the upcoming days and nights when he — and Pemberley — would be lonely and alone again.

∞∞∞∞

That she had never been in a more elegant, large, and comfortable bedchamber meant little to Elizabeth compared to the spectacular sight that lay in front of her eyes. He had been so generous as to allow her a place in his home, despite her calling him the last man in the world, and his generous and forgiving character added more pain to her feeling of loss. As she had told him already, she did not regret refusing him *then*, as her feelings for him had not been appropriate at that time. But she deeply regretted misjudging him so utterly and missing the chance to even recognise and understand his true character.

She had denied herself a chance at happiness which might or might not be offered to her again. If he did ever propose to her a second time, it would be further proof of his many qualities, to which the steadiness of his feelings would be added, but that would not absolve her of lack of wit and faulty reasoning.

A knock on the door interrupted her musings, and Mrs Gardiner entered, elegantly attired and glowing with delight.

"Oh Lizzy, my dear, I still cannot believe this is happening! I am staying in the family wing at Pemberley! Have you seen the view? As a child, in Lambton, I often wondered about the people in these rooms, and now I am one of them. If it never happens again, I shall still treasure these days for the rest of my life."

"I confess that was the subject of my reflections too. I am a little overwhelmed."

"Lizzy, my love, you must tell us the truth! We have been meaning to ask you since the first day we happened upon Mr Darcy. Do you and Mr Darcy have some sort of understanding? Such peculiar attention cannot come from mere friendship, and you cannot continue to pretend that it does."

"My dear aunt, I assure you that there is no understanding between us. But I shall not deny that Mr Darcy and I had a conversation about our friendship, and I am grateful that he holds me in high regard. But we cannot speak of anything more than friendship yet! And please do not even mention it in writing to my mother or father, as there is nothing to say!"

"Oh my dear, you may depend on my secrecy. And your uncle's. But Lizzy, what about you? What are your feelings?"

"My feelings? Oh, this is so complicated! I am ashamed of everything I have said about Mr Darcy in the past and even more so of what I believed about him. And I am thrilled and grateful for everything that is happening now," she admitted. The words expressed little of her feelings, but it was not the time for a longer discussion. Nor did Mrs Gardiner need more.

"I am so happy to hear that, my love. There is nothing I would like more than to see you and Jane happy in blissful marriages of love, as you deserve!" Mrs Gardiner concluded while taking Elizabeth's arm to walk downstairs.

At dinner, Mr Bingley immediately secured a seat near Elizabeth, eager to speak more to her about his own agenda. Darcy sat at one end of the table, with Miss Darcy on his right as always, and Mr Gardiner on his left. Mrs Gardiner and Mrs Annesley followed, and Miss Bingley and Mrs Hurst towards the other end of the table, of their own choice. Mr Hurst sat between his wife and Mr Bingley, as silent and as preoccupied with his glass and dishes as always.

"Miss Bennet, have you heard from your family recently?" Mr Bingley asked.

"No, I have not. I wrote to Jane before we arrived in Derbyshire, and I should receive her reply soon."

"Well, it might have already arrived, and you will find it tomorrow when you return to the inn," Miss Bingley said with feigned politeness.

"Will you stay longer in Derbyshire?" Mrs Hurst enquired. "It would be a shame to leave without receiving your letter."

Elizabeth smiled, amused by the sisters' rather obvious sting, and replied accordingly.

"We are not sure of our plans yet. Derbyshire proved to be even more beautiful, more agreeable than we expected, and for the moment, we are fully enjoying our time here."

"Speaking about plans," Mr Bingley interjected, "I spoke to Mr Gardiner today, and I might change mine. Darcy, would you mind if I left Pemberley sooner?"

"Leave Pemberley? What on earth for?" Miss Bingley cried.

"Because I want to return to Netherfield, of course. As I have already decided and informed you."

"Charles, have you considered what *we* want? How can you be so insensitive as to ruin our entire summer?" Mrs Hurst scolded him.

"I am sorry, but I cannot live my entire life considering what you want! I have done that too many times. I will leave Pemberley together with Mr and Mrs Gardiner. It will be more pleasant to travel together. If you wish to join us, so much the better. If not, we shall make other arrangements for the three of you to return safely and comfortably."

"This is outrageous!" Miss Bingley exclaimed, enraged. "We shall discuss this more tomorrow, in private, as such debates are not to be carried out in the presence of strangers."

"There are no strangers here, Caroline. Regardless, my decision is made. I apologise to Darcy and Miss Darcy for curtailing my visit, but if nothing else interferes with our plans, my stay at Pemberley this year will be very short."

"Bingley, we shall respect your decision, whatever it might

be. Do not worry about upsetting us, you should act only in a manner that makes you happy. And of course, I shall make all the necessary arrangements for your family to return to London whenever they wish, safely and comfortably."

"I shall surely not remain here if Bingley and Gardiner both leave," Mr Hurst suddenly interjected, much to everyone's surprise. "No offence, but Darcy is not too entertaining by himself. Besides, it is clear that Darcy has only ever invited us because Bingley is his friend. In his absence, it would be impolite to outstay our welcome!"

"Mr Hurst!" his wife cried, appalled.

"Hurst, I assure you that you are all welcome to stay as long as you like, with or without Bingley," Darcy intervened politely, although surprised by Mr Hurst's sudden insight.

"Thank you, but you are too busy a man to be bothered with entertaining. We may as well join Bingley in Hertfordshire. I quite enjoyed Netherfield. We might find some places to catch fish there too, or at least go shooting."

"Mr Hurst!" his wife cried again, in a scolding tone.

"Mrs Hurst! My decision is made too," Mr Hurst raised his voice with a severe tone that stunned and silenced the ladies in his family. "Could we eat now? I am starving."

The dinner continued rather awkwardly, with everyone trying to overcome the discomfort caused by the Bingleys' disagreement.

Miss Bingley and Mrs Hurst withdrew in angry silence, throwing sharp glares at everyone and especially at Elizabeth, whom they blamed for their humiliating rebuke by Mr Hurst of all people. Elizabeth felt embarrassed on their behalf and pitied them too much to even rejoice in their abasement, but in her mind, she applauded Mr Bingley's determination in standing up for himself.

By the second course, Mr Bingley was already engaged in animated conversation with Mr Gardiner, and Mr Hurst had already enjoyed a third glass of wine.

Elizabeth was seated rather far from Mr Darcy, and she barely spoke to him again, but their gazes met often. Words were not necessary yet; the important ones had been already spoken earlier in the carriage, and in addition, his attentiveness was more eloquent than any statement.

What Elizabeth and Darcy shared and were fearful to admit was the awareness that their time together would come to an end soon, that it was only one evening, one night, one morning, and after that, the future was unclear. She could do nothing but wait for a sign, a gesture, a word from him, while he was still affected by the recollection of his past failure to dare act too soon and too hastily.

After dinner, the gentlemen requested the favour of some music. Visibly not in the mood to perform or show their accomplishments, Mr Bingley's sisters declined, so Miss Darcy and Elizabeth indulged the party for half an hour.

As soon as propriety allowed, the sisters excused themselves and retired for the night. Miss Darcy declared she was tired, and she withdrew to her chamber too, with Mrs Annesley joining her.

The rest of the party remained, and all the tension vanished among them. The conversation flourished, with even Mr Hurst involved in it. At a convenient moment, Darcy sat on the sofa next to Elizabeth, a gesture without apparent significance but with much weight for both of them.

Various subjects were touched on and debated, always in light tones, with teasing, bantering, and mutual entertainment.

It was long after midnight when the party finally separated, and each moved to their rooms.

For Elizabeth, there were a few more minutes of delight, as Darcy joined them as they walked towards the family wing. He accompanied them to their chambers, where he bowed, bid them good night, and walked to his own rooms.

Elizabeth remained in the hall a moment longer, noticing his apartment was in the opposite corner but on the same hall. He seemed to feel her eyes upon him, knowing she was still gazing, so he glanced back at her, and she hurried inside her room, blushing, her heart beating wildly.

The distance between their rooms was significant, but she felt it was very close to her. Imagining him preparing for bed, wearing only his night clothes — did he wear a night shirt when sleeping? — the image of him lying in his bed, the realisation that she could have been in the mistress's apartment just next to his or even…if she had accepted his proposal... All those reflections made her by turns burning hot and shivering. Restless, she turned often from one side to the other and remained awake for a long while, too hot and bothered to sleep, even though she only wore a sheer nightgown and kept the window open.

From the hall, she heard some noises, creaks, and even some steps — very likely servants. From outside, the sounds of the summer night entered through the open window. Unable to lie down, she paced the room for a while, stepped onto the small balcony, admired the night sky and the moon's reflection, and finally returned to bed, struggling to sleep.

Not far away, Darcy was fighting with an even stronger storm of feelings, Elizabeth's nearness stirring his senses like never before. The thought of her, in bed, so close to him and yet... He was torn between happiness and fear of disappointment, hopes and fear of loss, exhaustion and excitement.

It was late in the night when he eventually fell into a deep sleep, but it did not last long; he woke up at dawn, startled from a dream that he could not remember. He remained in his room for a while, then he realised it was no use trying to fall asleep again, so he dressed without waking his man and prepared for the day.

As he walked towards the stairs, he heard steps and looked back, only to find Elizabeth just behind him, as though his thoughts had conjured her.

"Miss Bennet!"

"Mr Darcy!"

"Is anything amiss? Are you unwell?"

"I am perfectly well, thank you, but I could not sleep. I intended to look for a book or take a short walk until the others wake up," she replied, feeling uneasy.

"Good, we are in the same predicament then. I could not sleep either," he said. "Allow me to escort you to the library. Would you like a cup of tea? Some coffee, perhaps? I shall ask for a tray to be brought immediately."

"Yes, thank you," she answered, her heart light with joy but still somewhat embarrassed being in his company in such private circumstances when the household was mostly still asleep. She was not worried about being alone with him, but about enjoying their intimacy too much.

"And if you wish to take a walk afterwards, I would be happy to accompany you. If you approve of it, of course…"

"I do…very much," she answered, her glance meeting his for an instant before he opened the library door and invited her in.

Chapter 7

Being alone in the library at such an early hour was at the edge of propriety, but it was delightful enough to make them disregard the strict rules of decorum with little thought.

A servant entered soon with some coffee for the master, and he was asked to bring tea for Elizabeth too.

"This library is stunning. Exceptional," Elizabeth said. "Now I understand why you said you were proud of it. You certainly have every reason to be."

He smiled as she quoted his words from one evening at Netherfield. She seemed to remember their past encounters as well as he did.

"I am glad you approve of it, Miss Bennet."

"How could I not? Everything I have seen so far has been exceptional at Pemberley. I am grateful for the privilege of being here, Mr Darcy," she said genuinely, though slightly embarrassed at how her praises could be interpreted.

"And I am grateful for the joy of having you here, Miss Bennet," he replied with the same honesty, and her embarrassment increased, but her pleasure was doubled.

Fortunately, a maid entered with a tray of tea and biscuits, helping them to regain some composure. The cups were filled, and then the servant left. They enjoyed the drinks in silence, only glancing at each other. The peaceful moment spent alone, in Pemberley's library, early in the morning when the sun was just starting to kiss the high windows, was something that neither of them would have believed possible a short while ago, but both could easily imagine as a scene repeated in the future.

"I believe this is one of the most beautiful mornings I remember in a long while," he said, sipping from his coffee.

"I have no doubt it is," she answered, holding her teacup. "The view from the library is as lovely as the one from my room. Stunning," she repeated. "Thank you so much for providing us with those specific rooms. I could have stayed out on the balcony for days!"

"I am glad you enjoyed yourself. I hoped you would... You slept well, I hope?"

"I could not say," she admitted with a shy smile. "I was so restless all night that I cannot remember any sleep. But it was a good restlessness. The best I can ever remember."

"I did not sleep much either," he admitted. "I was thinking...Miss Bennet, I do not want to intrude or invade your privacy but...if you feel comfortable, I would be delighted if you stayed at Pemberley for the remainder of your visit to Derbyshire. You and your uncle and aunt," he said with a mixture of hope and restraint but also fear of asking too much.

Elizabeth blushed, blinking repeatedly and frowning slightly, flattered by another extraordinary gesture and fearful to read too much into it. Why was she so fearful?

"Please do not hesitate to refuse if I am being too intrusive! I asked because this is what I wish for, but you should only do as you please and feel comfortable with. I assure you I shall not mind either way."

"You are not being too intrusive, Mr Darcy. You know enough of my frankness to be certain I would speak if I found you so! I am just stunned and speechless. I know my uncle and aunt would be thrilled. But are you sure we are not the ones intruding, sir? Would the situation be agreeable for Miss Darcy? I know some of your other guests loathe our presence here."

"Miss Bennet, please never believe your presence is anything other than a pleasure to me. I have told you before and you know me well enough to believe I would not have said it, were it not true. My sister is already enjoying your company exceedingly. As for my other guests, I am trying to be a good host to everyone. That is why I suggested and allowed them the liberty to do anything that makes them happy. But I am the master of the house, and I will not ask permission for what makes *me* happy."

She smiled at him while sipping daintily from her cup. "Then, if my uncle and aunt agree, I shall accept your invitation with pleasure," she responded, her cheeks flushed with delight and her heart racing with high emotions.

The sound of the door being opened again broke the silence, and Mrs Annesley entered, stepping into the room without knocking or even asking permission.

"Mr Darcy, I beg your pardon for bursting in and

disturbing you, but…I went to Miss Darcy to help her prepare for the day, and she is not in her room." The lady looked flustered and highly alarmed, and Darcy frowned.

"Not in her room? She must have gone for a ride before breakfast. She has done so on occasion in the past. I shall send a servant to ask at the stables right away."

"No, I…I do not think she took a ride, sir…" the woman continued, glancing at Elizabeth as though she feared to speak freely.

"What do you mean, Mrs Annesley? Tell me at once what has happened!" Darcy demanded.

"I found this note on her pillow…In it, Miss Darcy says I should not worry about her and that she has left you a letter on your desk in the library…"

With a sudden change of countenance, Darcy almost jumped to his desk and rummaged around the spread papers with desperate haste until he found the one he was looking for. He opened it in a hurry and started to read, shaking his head and clenching his fists.

"This cannot be…" he whispered. "It cannot be," he repeated, putting the letter down, then grabbing it again. Elizabeth watched mesmerised as his face displayed an array of feelings she had only seen once before, that day at the parsonage. She stood, a lump in her throat and her heart a shard of ice in her breast from anguish.

Mrs Annesley was now extremely pale, and her voice trembled with tears as she dared ask, "Sir…is Miss Darcy harmed in any way?"

The question seemed to shake Darcy from his stupor, and

he looked at the two women with evident confusion.

"No...no...she is not harmed...Mrs Annesley, I would ask of you to return to your chamber for the moment. I shall speak to you later. Please do not mention anything to others about my sister's absence. If someone inquires, I shall tell them she is still in her room, indisposed, with a cold or fever or...I shall think of something. Please keep it private for now." He spoke quickly, with an obviously perturbed mind, one fist over his mouth while holding the letter tight in the other.

"Of course, Mr Darcy. As you say...please let me know how I may help."

"Only by doing as I asked, Mrs Annesley. Thank you, please leave me now..."

The woman exited, stepping hesitantly as though her knees were too weak. When the door closed, Darcy looked at Elizabeth for a long, intense moment, then sat in his armchair and clenched both his fists, the paper forgotten in one of them.

Without much consideration, Elizabeth pulled up a chair and sat right in front of him, gently touching his arm.

"Sir, what has happened? Something must be very wrong, I can see that. You look very ill. May I fetch you something? A glass of wine, perhaps? Something stronger? Or perhaps tea?"

"No, no...I could probably drink something, but it would not help..." He caught her worried stare and replied while trying to swallow the lump in his throat.

"My sister has left me...all of us...and thrown herself into the arms of Wickham."

Elizabeth was so shocked that her eyes and mouth

widened, and she started to mumble.

"Wickham? But when? How? Where is she? I am sure he took her by force! What can be done? Let us go after her immediately! I shall fetch my uncle! And Mr Bingley!"

Elizabeth was so astonished, so agitated that she lost control of herself. She rose to her feet immediately and started for the door, but Darcy stood and grabbed her hand, keeping her still a moment longer while replying in a low voice.

"I do not know what can be done. She left with him willingly, undoubtedly by design. Her letter is very clear. She has been communicating with him for months now…she claims he has shown her proofs of his love and loyalty and care, and that he is the only man she could be happy with…"

"But…no! This cannot be! She could never be happy with such a man!" Elizabeth cried, wondering why Darcy looked calm and still as though he was incapable of moving.

"She specifically asked me to not follow her," he continued. "You may read for yourself," he said, handing her the crumpled piece of paper. "She asked me to show her my affection by respecting her choice and her chance at happiness. She said they would go to Gretna Green to marry immediately. She claims my father would have approved of this marriage and even mentioned to her years ago that he hoped she would find a husband like George. And she says I cannot understand her because I do not know the meaning of love…" he concluded, his last words barely audible.

Devastation washed over him and made him stagger like an intoxicated man.

The same last words fell like blades, taking Elizabeth's breath away. She cast a glance at him, but he was already moving towards the window, leaving her to read the letter. "This cannot be," she muttered to herself and almost threw the offending piece of paper away only to start it again from the beginning.

As she read the letter, Elizabeth understood that Georgiana had written it some time ago but only placed it on her brother's desk when the elopement occurred. The plan, of which the letter was only a part, had been laid long before. But some of the words written did not sound right to Elizabeth. As little as she knew Miss Darcy, she doubted the girl, at the age of sixteen, would dare tell her older brother, twelve years her senior, that he did not know the meaning of love. Or mention their father several times in reference with such a subject. Elizabeth could simply not imagine that it was something a girl of her age and with her disposition would do.

She put the letter — a slip of paper holding the power to change so many lives — back on the table and glanced towards the window against which Darcy leant. She watched his uncharacteristically defeated posture and slumped shoulders for several minutes, not wanting to interrupt his thoughts, until he eventually turned away from the window, looking expectant, waiting for her impressions. For a long moment, Darcy and Elizabeth simply stared at each other, both too astonished to utter a single word, the letter lying open on the table, a sudden barrier between them.

The light-hearted delight and joy that had brightened their morning had swiftly turned into confusion and incredulity, the exhilaration into anger and guilt, just like dark clouds had suddenly covered the sun. She found the fortitude to break the heavy silence — but what could be said when so much was felt? What use might there be for words when feelings were so strong?

"I cannot fathom it... I know what we read, I understand the words, yet some of them I cannot comprehend..." Elizabeth finally whispered. "How is it possible? How could one dare…?"

"I…I would have never expected this…" Darcy swallowed thickly and continued more resolutely, "It is my fault alone. I allowed it to happen. I should have taken measures long ago."

"No, you cannot blame yourself, Mr Darcy. No more than I blame myself for my poor judgment and ridiculous misplaced trust," Elizabeth replied, fighting tears of shame and helplessness.

"I can and I do, Miss Bennet. I am to blame for this and much more. If only…" He hit his fist on the table, and the sound was as frightening as his dark countenance. Elizabeth startled and gasped, taking a step back.

He noticed and immediately turned to her, his voice changing utterly. "Forgive me, I did not mean to scare you. I shall find a way to remedy my wrongs, I promise. I will find a way to resolve it. That, I may promise you and myself," he vowed.

"I am not scared, and I trust you will do everything that is possible and beyond. Yet before that, sir, if I may… Miss Darcy might have been persuaded and eloped by design. I cannot doubt that, since she obviously took some actions by herself and over such a long period. It was all premeditated, and surely with her consented involvement. But…"

"But?" he asked, torn between desolation and a glimmer of hope.

"Parts of this letter do not sound like Miss Darcy wrote them, at least not freely. It feels like someone has dictated some of the sentences, someone who knows how heavily they will weigh in *your* decision regarding future actions against them."

"I fail to understand you, Miss Bennet."

"You see, in the letter...here, for instance — the claim that your father mentioned to Georgiana that he would wish for her to find a husband like Wickham — surely this must be a fabrication! Wickham must have asked her to write it. Your sister was ten years old when your father passed away, if I remember correctly. Would your father speak of marriage to his daughter at that age and, seemingly, even earlier? And that reference to you not knowing the meaning of love," she added, blushing as a fresh wave of guilt and remorse passed over her. "No young lady with Miss Darcy's sensible nature and gentle education would say that to her older brother! It simply cannot be!"

His interest seemed to increase, and his attention focused more. He stepped towards her, only inches away.

"What do you mean, Miss Bennet? Forgive me, but my mind is clouded. I am trying to think of a way to conceal this tragic situation from public knowledge until I have more details. I must protect as much as I can of Georgiana's peace and reputation, although I know not much will be possible, and not for long."

"Yes, I understand that. I believe it is the right thing to do — to keep the entire matter secret until there is a resolution to it. What I meant is that Mr Wickham did persuade your sister, but with more deception and lies. I am ashamed to admit that I sense in her letter the same sentiments of compassion and complete trust that I entertained for that man a while ago. I believe I know how he did it, and perhaps it is not too late to change her decision."

"What do you mean?" he insisted. "Change her decision? They must be on their way to Gretna Green now and will be married in a few days. Even if I found her — should I forcefully pull her back and lock her away? Keep her under guard for a few years? Or perhaps I could simply shoot Wickham! My cousin suggested doing that last summer — I regret I did not listen to him!"

"I am sure he wishes to marry her as soon as possible because Miss Darcy has everything he has ever wanted and chased after: name, fortune, and connections. I think she wishes to marry him because she was led to believe he has many attractive qualities that he only feigned: affection, loyalty, earnestness, constancy, honour, and the desire to improve himself for her sake. He knows Miss Darcy only too well and knew how to manipulate her trust since he has known her since she was born. She knows too little of his true character, mostly from her fond memories as a child."

"True…"

"It is an unfair, purposely deceptive situation. Had she known the whole truth, had she been aware of his true nature and of his habit of seducing young women, she would not have agreed to even speak to him ever again!"

"You have sketched this tragic situation perfectly. Mayhap it was my fault for not revealing the whole truth to her. But how could I have related to my young sister Wickham's string of debauchery, seductions, deceptions, forcing himself on maids, gambling, drinking, and so many others? When? Last year before Ramsgate, she was not yet fifteen, I still thought her a child! I would certainly not have told her about any of these things even if she were older. This kind of behaviour is not for a gentle young lady's knowledge. Should I have told her that our father was wrong in his estimation? That Wickham used them both for his own purposes? He only let them both see what he wanted! It was in my presence he was less guarded…and now… now it is all too late. She will learn the painful truth when it is all too late! How could I allow that to happen? I was blind, and wrong again, only this time someone else will suffer from my misgivings."

"Nobody could fault you for trying to protect your innocent sister! Nobody would have imagined Wickham capable of such impertinent audacity. To keep in touch with her since last summer's attempt, after you ordered him, warned him to stay away! And the colonel as well. His insolence is even greater than the fear of repercussions."

"He must be in desperate need of money again. I should have known he was capable of anything for his own comfort and to exact revenge!"

"Dear Lord, what was I thinking?" he whispered almost to himself.

He pulled himself together, and after taking a deep breath, he spoke with fierce determination.

"I cannot allow this to happen! Reputation and name be damned, I must find her and stop her! I must bring her back home. Miss Bennet, forgive me, I must leave, I do not have another instant to lose."

She grasped his arm tightly, stopping him.

"Mr Darcy, only a moment, please. Let us calm down and decide the best course of action. You wish to follow them — I understand that! It is most important. But what about your guests? And how will you avoid the gossip spreading? Your name and Miss Darcy's reputation need not suffer. And what should I do?"

He stopped for a while, looking seriously at her. She was close to him, her face upturned, trying to convey her own determination with her eyes.

"You are correct yet again, Miss Bennet, and I apologise for my thoughtlessness, but I am so angry that I would probably shoot Wickham without a second thought if he happened to face my pistol! Regardless, this will turn into a great scandal that will be the talk of London and beyond. But as I said, name and reputation are less important to me now. I only hope to save my sister from a life of misery. You and your relatives should leave Pemberley at once and distance yourselves from me before your name is tarnished by association."

"Distance myself from you? You mistake me entirely, Mr Darcy, if you think that is what I meant! Nay, Sir! Quite the opposite — I am considering joining you in your quest! And if you hand me a pistol, I will readily shoot Mr Wickham myself!"

Elizabeth's determined statement stunned Darcy speechless for a few seconds. Was she joking? If so, it was an unfortunate moment. Was she being serious? It seemed rather impossible.

"Miss Bennet, that would be unacceptable, of course. I thank you for your care, but I cannot allow you to expose yourself further to this situation. I shall remedy this mistake by myself."

"Sir, hear me for a moment. You should not go alone — you could ask either Mr Bingley or my uncle to join you. They are both trustworthy people, loyal to you. But in order to better control this situation and the possibility of word being spread, Mr Bingley should maybe take care of his sisters. Perhaps he might be persuaded to return to London immediately, taking his sisters with him? You know him well enough to decide whether you can tell him the truth, but not them. My uncle is an excellent man who I trust with my life. Since Wickham has only seen him on one occasion and for a very short time, he might be useful to your search."

She braced herself, turned her chin up a little, and looking him in the eye, spoke with all the assurance she could muster. "And I want to come too."

Speaking thus, Elizabeth — with a clearer mind in the heat of the moment but equal care for Darcy and his sister — realised her suggestions piqued Darcy's interest and curiosity, so she continued reasonably, "I would be of use to you too. If you find Miss Darcy and speak to her, in her highly emotional state she might not believe you, let alone listen to you. She might assume that you fabricated some of the stories you accuse Wickham of, only to scare and separate her from him. But *I* can tell her — even in the presence of Wickham! — of everything I know about his attempts to pursue Mary King for her dowry, and all the accusations he made against you. In these difficult circumstances, she might believe me more than you."

Darcy listened to every word but was far from agreeing. He did trust Bingley and Mr Gardiner and understood he might not succeed without their support. But exposing Elizabeth to any danger was unacceptable to him. Still, some of her ideas had merit.

"These are worthy notions, and I thank you. Yet, I am not sure…It all sounds like a horrible mistake with no good solution. I shall send for Bingley. Can you please ask your uncle and aunt to join us? If we take this course of action, I shall also tell Mrs Reynolds the truth. She must know, in order to keep the servants under good regulation."

A quarter of an hour later, on a morning that had started like a dream but turned into the worst misery imaginable, Elizabeth had relayed the shocking news to the stunned Gardiners, and all three of them approached the library, where Mr Darcy and Mr Bingley were engaged in a heated discussion.

"I have already informed my uncle and aunt — briefly," Elizabeth said.

"And I have spoken to Bingley, as you suggested," Darcy replied.

"I shall speak to my sisters immediately. I shall inform them that Miss Darcy has caught an illness — probably from the tenants — and she might be contagious. I shall convey that the doctor insisted she should not be in company for at least a week and that it would be safest for us to leave Pemberley immediately. My sisters will not question it any further."

Mr Bingley made the statement with such seriousness and gravity that nobody could doubt his words.

"I am ready to join you on your journey to Gretna Green, Mr Darcy," Mr Gardiner said. "If anybody asks, I am going to visit some distant relatives and am taking my niece with me."

"Do you think that would be wise, Mr Gardiner? Would Mr Bennet approve?" Darcy asked with legitimate concern.

"I take full responsibility for that, Mr Darcy. I shall make arrangements for my wife to remain in Lambton, to spend more time with her own relatives until we return."

"I may also help Mrs Annesley and Mrs Reynolds if they need my assistance," Mrs Gardiner intervened.

Darcy paced the library, thinking and over thinking everything they knew and had been discussed. He was agitated, uncertain of his actions and decisions as he rarely had ever been. But he could not think of another course of action for now, and time was being wasted.

"So — all is settled? We are all in agreement?" he asked,

glancing at his companions.

"All is settled. We shall all return to the inn now. Oh, and Mr Darcy? Perhaps we should travel in my carriage so it will not be recognised if we happen upon Wickham?" Mr Gardiner suggested. "It is not so large, nor so elegant or comfortable as yours, but it can easily accommodate four people. You may, however, take another coachman, besides mine."

"Good idea! Good thinking! Excellent!" Mr Bingley readily approved. "Well then, goodbye for now. I am going to wake and hurry my sisters to prepare for the journey. I shall wait for good news, Darcy. And I hope to see you all soon at Netherfield," he addressed the Gardiners. "Oh, and Darcy? Shoot that damn bastard! Not to kill him, perhaps in the leg, or shoulder. Enough to make him suffer for at least a month before he recovers."

Mr Bingley's outburst was completely out of character, as it was hard to believe such words of violence could have come out of his mouth. But — as surprised as they were — everyone in the library agreed with him heartily.

Not one full hour later, the Gardiners and Elizabeth were returned to the inn, Mr Bingley had explained the situation and demanded his sisters make haste and gather their things, while Darcy was deep in conversation with Mrs Reynolds and his loyal valet. A small trunk was already waiting, and on top of it, in a closed chest, was a pistol.

Chapter 8

Mr Gardiner's carriage picked up Darcy and his trusted man from the meeting point — the fishing stream. Darcy seemed slightly surprised at seeing Elizabeth, as though he had assumed she would not join them after all. He sat on the bench opposite them, said, 'Thank you," and then was silent for a while.

"How long will it take us to reach Gretna Green?" Elizabeth asked.

"I would say around three days. Am I wrong, Mr Darcy?" Mr Gardiner replied. "We shall have to rest for two nights. I hope we can find some decent inns on the road."

"You are correct, sir," Darcy said. "There is a reliable inn, where I have personally stayed before, in Preston, fifty miles away. The Old Dog. The problem is we left Pemberley very late so, even with the benefit of a long summer day, I doubt we could cover the distance before it gets dark. So, we shall have to look for an inn in Manchester tonight. Wickham is probably a few hours ahead of us, but no doubt he thought he would have even more time."

"But Mr Darcy, we should press on for as long as necessary!" Elizabeth protested. "The longer we travel tonight, the better chance we have of reducing their lead and catching them!"

"Perhaps, but I cannot agree to travel during the night. I will not put your safety at risk, Miss Bennet, nor Mr Gardiner's."

Elizabeth tried to argue, but Darcy continued decidedly, "We may leave tomorrow morning very early if that is acceptable to you both. And I trust we can ride faster than them, as we can change horses whenever necessary. We have two coachmen, so we do not need to rest at all during the day but stop for refreshments only. However, I would like to stop at the main inns on the road anyway and enquire as to whether Wickham and my sister have been seen."

"Of course, that would be the best course of action," Mr Gardiner agreed. As for asking at the inns, we should claim Wickham is a friend and we plan to meet him but are uncertain of his whereabouts."

"Good thinking," Darcy said.

"Sir, may I ask…do you know when they left Pemberley? And do you happen to know whether Miss Darcy took anything valuable with her? Has her maid noticed anything? Can we safely assume Wickham will have enough money on him?" Mr Gardiner continued.

"I would guess that they left last night, at the very latest at dawn. We retired rather late, as you know. He certainly was aware we had guests. They must have waited until the entire household retired and were sure all had fallen asleep. As for my sister, yes, I assume she took her pin money. I never check how much money she possesses or how she uses it. But as she has not had many occasions to spend any, I can, unfortunately, suppose it is much of it."

"Therefore, he might change horses rather often, too," Mr Gardiner uttered. "There goes an advantage I thought we had on him. Hence, we may gain some time only by reducing our resting time as much as possible, without neglecting our safety."

"That would be a correct conclusion, Mr Gardiner. I…"

"Yes?" Elizabeth encouraged him, seeing as Darcy seemed troubled by a sudden thought.

"In the event we do find them before reaching Gretna Green…what should I do? Can I just grab my sister and force her to come home against her will? If I did that, even though it is my prerogative as her guardian, even though it is for her well-being and future happiness, will she ever forgive me? I might save her from a life of misery and grief, but what if I lose her affection, trust, and respect forever?"

The man known as the best master and landlord, who took care of so many others depending on him, who was always self-confident and in charge of everything, used to making decisions for everyone and to whom everyone turned for counsel, was asking for advice. He appeared vulnerable, exposing his deepest fears and doubts. Any traces of pride, arrogance, or disdain were long gone.

"It is to your credit that you care so much for your sister's feelings, Mr Darcy. You may at least talk to her and be certain it is really her wish," Elizabeth answered with warmth and sympathy. "You should reveal to her everything that was kept hidden until now, so she may make an informed decision."

"Everything…even what might hurt her?" Darcy repeated.

"Yes," Elizabeth answered. "You believe you are protecting your sister from the pain caused by the truth. But without it, the pain caused by ignorance might be even stronger and last for a lifetime."

"I am not going to argue with you, Miss Bennet. I know you are right, and I am grateful for your support."

Engrossed in his own thoughts, Darcy was in no disposition for conversation, and the other two respected his privacy, occupying themselves with reading or speaking in soft tones to each other. The carriage kept up a hasty pace, the turning of the wheels and the clatter of the horses' hoofs being the loudest sounds. They were on a quest that had only a slim chance of being successful. What troubled everyone but nobody dared voice was the fear that Miss Darcy may have already been intimate with the scoundrel and — the worst outcome — that there might even be consequences. In such circumstances, whether she decided to marry him or not, her life would be ruined, and the scandal polluting Darcy's name would be unavoidable; but it would be the guilt that would burden Darcy that would be unbearable.

They eventually made their first stop at an inn to change horses and eat something in haste.

The next hours passed mostly in awkward silence. Elizabeth looked out through the window, watching places pass that she had never seen before, but for the first time she was not captivated and did not enjoy the view. Unlike her usual self while travelling, she had little curiosity and interest in her surroundings, so preoccupied was she with Darcy and his sister. His concern and sadness etched lines of worry on his handsome face and broke her heart.

"Mr Darcy, have you been to this part of the country

before? I remembered you mentioned you had," Mr Gardiner attempted a conversation.

"Yes. Several times," the answer came curtly.

"It is beautiful, is it not, Lizzy?"

"Yes, it is…" she replied with such equal indifference that Mr Gardiner gave up the subject.

They continued until it was almost completely dark outside, and only then did they stop at the Wagon and Horses in Westhoughton, although Darcy was most reluctant to stay in an area where there were rumours about the Luddites being in full unrest.

Darcy hurried down from the carriage, helped Elizabeth to step out, and then rushed inside to speak to the innkeeper.

Elizabeth stretched, welcoming the standing position as her feet and back felt quite numb, and realised she had never ridden for so long without a break. She and Mr Gardiner followed Darcy while the two coachmen attended to the horses.

"They did not stop here," Darcy came to inform them. "Fortunately, the inn is rather empty, and there are enough spare rooms. I have asked for dinner to be sent to my room if that is convenient for you."

"Yes, of course," Mr Gardiner agreed.

"I have also asked for the service of a maid. She will show you to your chambers and assist you with everything you may need. I am going to check on the coachmen and will join you soon. Dinner should be ready in half an hour."

The tasks he had to accomplish, including seeing to his servants' comfort, brought back a glimpse of the Mr Darcy she had come to know. For the moment, his sense of duty had won over his own fears.

The maid showed Elizabeth to her room — simple but clean and large enough. She did not care about the details, and thanked the maid, assuring her she would ring if she needed anything. As soon as she was alone, she took off her bonnet, gloves, and spencer and lay on the bed. It too had clean sheets and felt very comfortable, and those were the only things she cared about, as tiredness started to engulf her. Without sleeping much the previous night, with all the emotion of the first hour of the morning and the torment that followed, as well as the long journey with only one hasty stop, Elizabeth could not decide whether she was more exhausted or hungry.

She let her thoughts run to Miss Darcy — who was surely in a similar inn somewhere. As little as she knew the girl and her relationship with her brother, Elizabeth believed she must surely be worried, fearful, and ashamed, and she wondered how much Wickham was taking advantage of her and how much, if at all, she was aware of it.

It was very likely that he would attempt to consummate a marriage that had not taken place yet, to be certain of his success and especially to gain the upper hand against Darcy. But would he dare force himself on her? Or was he relying on his power of seduction and charming ways? That notion sickened and enraged her at the same time. She recalled his practised smile which had beguiled her, as well as his tales of woe that she had believed — despicable, poor excuse for a man that he was!

"Lizzy? Dinner has been brought up," she heard Mr Gardiner calling her, and she arranged her appearance briefly, passing her palms over her wrinkled skirt and then checking her hair before she opened the door.

"Come my dear, we are starving," he said, leading her

towards the third room on the same floor.

Darcy was pacing the room, ignoring the table full of dishes. At their entrance, he invited them to sit before finally taking a chair himself.

"How early should we leave tomorrow?" he enquired, glancing at Elizabeth.

"As soon as you wish, sir. I shall be ready at dawn."

"Good. Miss Bennet, we have tea, but I also asked for some port to be brought up. Perhaps you would like a little? It would surely help you sleep better."

"Thank you, no. I am so tired that I shall sleep as soon as I lay my head on the pillow, and the port will only give me a headache. I shall retire to my chamber as soon as I have finished my dinner."

"As you wish. Our trunks should be being carried in as we speak. I also took the liberty of arranging for food for tomorrow. Mrs Reynolds insisted I should take a basket, as I always do when I travel, but in my haste to leave at once, I refused it. I have come to regret it since you had to suffer more discomfort because of me."

"Do not worry, Mr Darcy," Mr Gardiner replied. "What is important is that we have arrived here, as we planned. I shall pour myself some port — I know for sure it will help me to sleep better."

Dinner was rather quiet, and they spoke of little except some details about the next day's journey. They ate quickly, and as soon as her appetite was satisfied, Elizabeth excused herself and returned to her room, too tired to even keep her eyes open. The gentlemen remained, nursing drinks and sharing a tentative conversation.

∞∞∞

As planned, the first glimpse of light found Elizabeth already awake and ready for the ride. The maid knocked on her door, bringing hot water and tea, and helped her to get dressed quickly. Soon after, Mr Gardiner came to fetch her.

It was not yet full daylight when they started the second leg of their quest, and by the time the sun was up, they had long left Manchester behind.

"You two gentlemen look very ill," Elizabeth said after studying them both. "I am sorry to say that you look worse than you did last night!"

"It may well be true," Mr Gardiner answered, "considering we did not sleep much and spent the night talking. And drinking. Mr Darcy offered me some valuable advice, as I intend to purchase a small estate sometime in the future."

Elizabeth arched her brow in reproach. "It was very kind of Mr Darcy, but do you think it was an appropriate time for such a conversation? You look like you barely slept *at all*. We have another long day ahead of us, and you are already exhausted. Tonight, I shall check on each of you to be sure you are in your own bed immediately after dinner," she declared decidedly. Suddenly, she felt her face and neck burning, and she knew she was all flushed, as the image of Darcy in his night clothes and lying in his bed appeared, again uninvited, in her mind.

"You do not have to do that, Lizzy. I am sure the

exhaustion will get the better of us by then, after we have travelled another sixty miles."

Darcy chose to not reply, but Elizabeth could see a little smile, a shadow of a smirk really, in the corner of his mouth, and she wondered whether he was thinking of her checking on him at bedtime.

In Preston, Darcy questioned the innkeeper about Wickham and Georgiana, and, after slipping the man a few coins, he found out they had stayed there the previous night.

Three hours later, when they reached another inn, Darcy again enquired after the fugitives whilst Elizabeth and her uncle stretched their legs for a short while.

"They have not passed here," Darcy explained when they were back in the carriage. "Wickham must have chosen another route to avoid the main road."

"Are there other routes?" Elizabeth asked. "And how does Wickham know that?"

"Wickham...let me just say it is not the first time he has done this, nor the first time that I have. Chased after him, I mean, of course. A couple of months after my father died, he attempted to elope with the niece of my aunt, Lady Matlock. She was only seventeen years old. Two years later, he tried the same scheme, this time with the daughter of a successful tradesman who owns several shops in Manchester and in London," Darcy explained, as mortified as if he was to blame.

Elizabeth and her uncle were stupefied.

"How is it possible? Is this man real?" Mr Gardiner voiced their incredulity. "In truth, it is strange that nobody has shot him before now! And Lizzy, I cannot believe you and all the people in Meryton were so fooled and thought so highly of him!"

"It is a shame that will not pass soon, Uncle. I feel I am accountable for the good opinion others had of him too, since I was the first he spoke to. The first simpleton he chose to fool, to work for him by spreading the rumours further. He could not have chosen better!" she mocked herself dejectedly. "How stupid have I been?"

"You are too hard on yourself, Miss Bennet. If it were not for you, Wickham would have found other ways to propagate his falsehoods," Darcy intervened, not wanting to let Elizabeth feel guilty on his behalf. "I should have exposed him a long time ago, but it was the memory of my father, and for that matter of his own father as well, that stopped me. And now, my sister, my own sister has to suffer the consequences."

"Mr Darcy, given this new information, I must disagree with your initial plan," Mr Gardiner said. "I know I have no say in your decision, as ultimately it is you who are responsible, but I believe you should not allow Miss Darcy the liberty of choice! We should simply take her away, and you will have plenty of time to reveal the truth to her and to deal with Wickham afterwards. There is truly no choice when we speak of such a man!"

"Or I could just shoot him," Darcy said, half in jest.

"Well, that would be an excellent second plan," Mr Gardiner answered in all honesty. "Although, if you did shoot him, we would be delayed at least a couple of days before returning to Derbyshire, so I would rather avoid that unless it is absolutely necessary."

"A wise observation," Darcy replied after feigning serious consideration.

∞ ∞ ∞

After their second day of travelling, they managed to reach Kirkby-Lonsdale, covering about sixty miles in one day. They found available rooms, but again no trace of Wickham and Georgiana.

Like the previous night, they dined in Darcy's room, sharing their concerns.

"Could it be possible that something has happened to delay them?" Mr Gardiner asked. "Could they be behind us?"

"It is possible, but I doubt it. Regardless, we should still plan to leave tomorrow at dawn and travel as far as Carlisle. Everybody stops there on their way to Gretna Green. There are two or three good inns in Carlisle, and many others less respectable, not to mention the boarding houses, so I must enquire in each of them."

"I shall help you, of course," Mr Gardiner offered.

"The problem is that it is around sixty miles from here to Carlisle and ten more to Gretna Green. I fear it may be too tiring for Miss Bennet, so I shall go ahead on horseback, and you may rest another night on the road."

"Surely you are joking, Mr Darcy, because you know how dearly I love to laugh! Why would you assume it is too tiring for me to sit in a carriage? We have come all this way to offer you at least the assistance of keeping you company, and that is what we shall do. Besides, I would not miss the confrontation with Wickham even if I had to walk there!"

Darcy smiled at her allusion to another of their exchanges at Netherfield, but laughed at the end of her impassioned speech — for the first time in three days.

"I know you are an excellent walker, but that would be too much even for you. However, I do understand your point."

"It is settled then. I hope you two will go to sleep early tonight," she said.

"We cannot go to sleep early, as it is already late, Lizzy," Mr Gardiner teased her.

"We shall," Darcy promised obediently.

As she had done the night before, Elizabeth retired to her room as soon as she had eaten. The inn was busy enough, and through the open windows the sound of voices and horses could be easily heard, so it took a while for Elizabeth to fall asleep.

A loud noise awoke her sometime later, and she was confused momentarily. Finding her bearings, she went to the window in search of a breeze to cool herself. She leant out and took in the animated scene below: all the people, carriages, horses, torches, talk, and laughter.

With a start, she noticed Darcy on the same floor but a few windows away, looking outside too. He observed her and acknowledged her with a simple wave of his hand.

She withdrew from the window with a strange fluttering in her stomach. She took a few steps into the room, sat on the bed, stood again almost immediately, then startled at the soft knock.

She moved towards the door and asked who it was. She knew the answer even before she opened the door and stared at her visitor.

"Mr Darcy…"

"Miss Bennet, forgive my intrusion, but I saw you at the window. May I enquire as to your health? Why are you not asleep at this hour? Are you unwell?"

"I am well, I have slept a little, but I was awakened by the uproar in the yard. However, may I ask why *you* are not asleep, Mr Darcy? That was a promise you have not kept," she teased him. He was in his indoor clothes — only loose soft trousers, a linen shirt, and a waistcoat. He looked pale, and his hair was rather untidy. She had never seen him like this, in his shirt sleeves, without a cravat and the top button of his shirt loose.

"I tried, but there was too much noise for me too. Miss Bennet, you left earlier and did not take anything with you. May I fetch you something to drink or something to eat? Some tea, some fruit? All the trays are yet in my chamber, and I may fetch you whatever you wish in an instant."

"Oh…I admit it is a rather warm night, and I am somewhat thirsty. Tea, even cold, would be nice, please. Or water. And some biscuits, if possible."

"Of course! Just a moment, please," he replied and hurried to his chamber, her eyes following him down the hall, marvelling again at the incongruity of their situation. Only then did Elizabeth recall she was wearing just her thin nightgown and her hair was loose on her shoulders. She hurried to put on a robe, then tightened it around her with a sash, just in time to see Darcy reappear with a small tray in one hand and a candle in the other.

"I took the liberty of bringing more than you asked for. Including a finger of port. Perhaps you will accept my suggestion tonight.

"Thank you, sir." She smiled as he entered the room, put the tray on the little table, and made to step back to the door.

"Would you like to stay a moment, sir? Perhaps partake of what you brought me? Have a drink and talk a little?" she asked daringly, fully aware her invitation was beyond improper.

She felt even more mortified when he answered, "Thank you, no. It is very late. I should not even be here. If anyone sees us, there will be even more talk. Besides, we both need to sleep."

"Of course, sir. As you wish," Elizabeth responded, lowering her eyes to the floor so he could not see that she felt like a fool facing his rejection.

"Miss Bennet..." she heard him calling her and eventually lifted her eyes to look at him.

He continued, his voice raspy, his eyes dark with exhaustion and perhaps something else too.

"Miss Bennet, it is not as I wish. There is nothing that I want more than your company, but I know I should not be here. I hope to hear such an invitation again sometime soon, in other circumstances, so I can feel free to respond differently."

Warm inside and shivering outside, her face still flushed but with glimmers in her eyes, Elizabeth nodded as he bowed and left. In the hall, he looked back at her one more time, then entered his room.

Elizabeth closed and locked the door, leaning against the heavy wood, heart racing and almost short of breath, reflecting on their brief almost illicit encounter, at what had just happened and what had been said. Then she sat at the table, smiled and happily picked up a few pieces of fruit from the tray, her eyes eventually falling on the small glass of port.

He had insisted twice already that she have a drink, and she had refused him once. She could not possibly refuse him twice, even if he was not there to witness it. So she took the glass and enjoyed it in small sips until she had finished it completely. The sweet, strong wine immediately made her dizzy, whilst the warmth inside her increased.

With hesitant steps, she returned to bed and lay back against the pillows, thinking of his words and blushing again. He had made the decision to leave against his wishes, visibly struggling, mindful of propriety.

'In vain I have struggled. It will not do. My feelings will not be repressed...'

Before she fell asleep, with her head spinning from the sweet port, Elizabeth wondered whether she still possessed the power to do something so he would never have to struggle against his feelings and wishes again.

Chapter 9

T he last day of their journey also started at dawn. Elizabeth had slept better than the first night, but it was still insufficient. After the brief encounter with Darcy, she had needed some time to soothe her nervousness, and thoughts about his sister had troubled her even longer. In the carriage, she noticed that her uncle looked rested, but Darcy's weariness and agitation increased as they were approaching the moment of the confrontation.

On their way, they made more enquiries about the fugitives, but there were still no positive answers. It could mean that Wickham had chosen only lesser-travelled routes, or that they had paid some of the innkeepers handsomely to not disclose their presence no matter who asked, or that they travelled with someone else, as Darcy speculated.

"Whatever has happened, they must stop in Carlisle tonight. It is already very late, and it would be of no use to them to arrive in Gretna Green at night," Darcy said hopefully. "If so, we shall discover them soon. I shall search every inn and every place that rents rooms in the whole of Carlisle."

"As I said, I shall help you, of course, so we can split the town in two," Mr Gardiner said. "We should book our rooms though, and while Lizzy remains there to rest, we can continue our quest on horseback."

"Yes, that sounds like a good plan," Darcy admitted.

"But you should be very careful, Mr Darcy, so they do not see you. They will recognise you straight away, but I am not so familiar."

"Wickham has only seen you once or twice, but Miss Darcy knows you well enough, Uncle," Elizabeth interjected. "And I could help too — perhaps I can take a carriage and look for them."

"Absolutely not!" Darcy said in a manner that was so overbearing that Elizabeth frowned her displeasure. "I apologise for my tone, Miss Bennet," he added, "but I cannot allow you to go out alone in an unknown place, even in a carriage. There are many dishonourable men in Carlisle, as well as in Gretna Green. I need to know you are safe at the inn, so I do not have to worry about you too."

Elizabeth felt uncomfortable, irritated, and even offended by his tone, but she tried to remain calm. Mr Gardiner immediately supported Darcy's opinion, asking her to not expose herself to any danger.

"Very well, be it as you wish. Although I am perfectly capable of taking care of myself and confronting scoundrels if needed."

Her determination brought a little smile to Darcy's worried countenance.

"I do not doubt that, Miss Bennet. I did not mean any disrespect or to imply you were not able. As I hope you know, I admire your abilities greatly. I am grateful for your help, and I value your opinions. You have proved clearer-minded than I when needed, and I am in your debt for even embarking on the quest for my sister so promptly."

"I understand your meaning, Mr Darcy." She abandoned her stubbornness. "I shall not be in your way, nor shall I add more to your present distress."

"I am glad we are all in agreement. Now — how do you decide on which inn we shall stay at, Mr Darcy? I understand this is not your first visit here either," Mr Gardiner asked, and the conversation continued with fewer emotions and more efficiency.

The sun was slowly going down when they arrived in Carlisle. Elizabeth was curious and fascinated by the bustle of people; the town was animated, and observing a certain person in all that agitation was not an easy task.

They booked rooms at the King's Head on Fisher Street, and Elizabeth asked to be given a chamber with windows that looked out towards the street. Darcy and Mr Gardiner refused any food or drink and, as had been discussed and agreed upon, left after a short while. Elizabeth remained in her room as promised, trying to rest, but the time passed, evening fell, and she still received no word.

Eventually, she wrote a short note and left it on the bed, then she went in search of her uncle's servant, John. The man was having a drink with his companion and was surprised to see her.

"How may I assist you, Miss Lizzy?"

"John, I would like to go for a walk. Would you be so kind as to keep me company? I promised my uncle I would not leave the inn alone."

"O' course, miss. But a walk? At this hour?"

"Yes, only for a little while and not too far."

"As you say, miss. May Tom come with us, miss?"

"Certainly," Elizabeth replied.

She then asked a maid who was serving drinks whether there were any other inns or places to rent a room nearby, as she was waiting for a friend and had heard there may be other establishments in the vicinity.

"But miss, they are nothing like our inn," the maid said with some pride. "Your friend cannot be there. No one of consequence would stay there, our inn is one of the best."

"I am sure you are right," Elizabeth said with friendly smile and an easy, encouraging manner. "And if my friend happens to be staying somewhere else, I shall certainly persuade her to move here."

"'Tis kind of you, miss. When should I bring your dinner? The tall gentleman paid for it earlier. He ordered a lot of food and drink, but only your coachmen have eaten."

"Please keep it ready until he and my uncle return. They have some urgent business yet. Oh, and if they return, tell them I went for a walk and will be back soon. I have left them a note."

"Will do, miss!"

With that, Elizabeth took the direction of the nearest

establishments with rooms, with the plan to check them by herself. She felt enthused by the endeavour and pleased that she could take part in the search instead of just languishing in her room. She walked at a slow pace as though she was taking a stroll, looking at the people, places, and shop windows, the two coachmen only steps behind, all their attention on her and the people on the street. The next inn was a short distance away, and once there, she asked the same question, about her friend and her betrothed.

"We 'ave many young women and their betrotheds, ma'am," a boy told her, grinning. "You see, we are close to Gretna Green, and everybody goes there to marry. What does your friend look like?"

"Well, not quite everybody. I am not," Elizabeth joked. "My friend is very young and very pretty, you would surely remember her. With blonde hair and blue eyes."

"I don't think we 'ave 'er, miss. But shall I send you word if she comes later?" the boy offered, his eyes already counting the coins he could get from such a service.

"Yes, please. I am staying at The King's Head. Do you know it?" The boy nodded eagerly. "But please do not tell her, I want to give her a pleasant surprise," Elizabeth said with a friendly smile, offering the lad a shilling. He stared in surprise at such generosity and bowed low to her, repeating that he would certainly let 'the kind miss' know.

While she was talking to the boy, Darcy's servant approached in a hurry and whispered to her abruptly.

"Miss, miss, I beg your pardon, but you have to come, I just saw Wickham!"

Elizabeth's heart skipped a beat, then raced as she followed the man outside.

"I pointed him out to John and let him follow, 'cause Wickham don't know him."

"Excellent thinking! Did you notice whether Miss Darcy was with him?"

"No, ma'am. He was with another man though, talking. He came from that way," Tom pointed with his thumb.

"Perhaps we may have some luck, after all," Elizabeth said, taking the servant's arm in an absent gesture. "The next inn should be down this street. Let us go and ask!"

They hastened their pace, and several minutes later, following the direction Tom indicated and asking around, they found the inn. It was a small one, rather crowded and noisy, with many people eating, drinking, and talking outside.

As she had done before, Elizabeth enquired about her friend with blonde hair and blue eyes and claimed secrecy, while paying a generous reward. She could not believe her ears when the maid confirmed the young lady was there, she had seen her, just arrived with her companion at sunset.

"So are they in the room as we speak?" Elizabeth asked, still doubting her chance.

"Yes, ma'am. Second floor, the second room on the right. I'll show you."

"Yes, that would be lovely. Just allow me a moment longer please, there is another friend I am waiting for before giving them a surprise."

In a very perturbed state of mind, Elizabeth wondered how to proceed. She could not confront them alone, nor allow either of them to see her. Tom had said that Wickham had left, so Miss Darcy might very well be alone. Would Wickham have enlisted someone else in his scheme like he had done with Mrs Younge? No, she did not think so. Perhaps she could take advantage of Wickham's absence to talk to the girl alone, but what if she refused? After all, Elizabeth was almost a stranger, someone outside Miss Darcy's circle, someone she would never befriend under different circumstances, and their acquaintance was too recent to have gained her trust and confidence. Since she had not listened to her brother and agreed to elope, defying every sensible argument and reason, without fearing the consequences of a scandal for her family, why would she even listen to someone so wholly unconnected to her? Elizabeth's attempt might cause more harm than help, so she hesitated to proceed further.

Outside, Tom was waiting for orders, which Elizabeth was not able to provide.

"Perhaps I should wait here, and you can go and fetch my uncle and Mr Darcy," Elizabeth asked, hoping that the man might have another suggestion. She could return to where she was staying, but she hesitated to do so on her own, nor could she remain where she was alone.

"The master will come here eventually if he checks every inn," Tom said. "Unless he has already been here before they arrived, but I don't think so."

The answer confused Elizabeth even more and forced her to decide.

"Tom, are you sure the man you saw was Mr Wickham?"

"On my life, miss. I have known that rascal — pardon me, miss — since he was a boy. I would recognise him from a mile away."

"Very well then. I am going to speak to Miss Darcy, if she is indeed in her room. Please remain here and keep watch. I trust you to help me handle this situation if necessary."

"Do not worry, miss. I will guard your life with mine."

With increased determination, Elizabeth climbed the stairs and knocked on the door, first timidly, and then when nothing happened, more strongly.

"Yes? Who is it?" At last she heard Miss Darcy's soft voice.

Disguising her voice as best she could, Elizabeth replied, "'Tis only I, miss. Janey the maid. I've brought you some tea."

"Oh...I...I cannot open the door...my... be-betrothed has left for only a short while, and he took the key."

"If you want me to, miss...I can open the door and leave you the tea?"

"I would like that, if you can, yes please."

"Just a moment, ma'am, I'll fetch the key!" Elizabeth replied, and then she ran down the stairs and asked the maid she had generously rewarded earlier to open the door. The young woman agreed after only a brief hesitation and another generous payment.

The maid unlocked the door then immediately left, leaving Elizabeth to face the occupant of the room. Upon opening the door, Miss Darcy gasped with astonishment and stepped back, while Elizabeth tried to act with more control than her agitation allowed.

"Miss Bennet! What are you doing here?"

"Miss Darcy...I am glad I have found you. I have come to talk to you. As a friend..."

"But...why? Dear Lord, how did you find me? Is my brother here too?" she cried in alarm and tried to look over Elizabeth's shoulder to see whether Darcy was behind her.

"Yes. Mr Darcy and my uncle are both here, searching for you."

The girl looked panicked and confused, so pale that Elizabeth feared she would faint. She stepped forward, then stopped at seeing the girl's dismay.

"Miss Darcy, your brother came only to talk to you and to be sure that you are safe. I insisted on joining him, but he said he would respect your decision, whatever it may be, if you are certain of it...and to be sure you know the full truth about the man you wish to share your life with."

"Miss Bennet, my brother always disliked and envied George! You know that. But George is a good and kind man. I know you were his friend too."

"I was his friend, yes, until I discovered Mr Wickham had not been honest with me. I am sorry to say that, and maybe you do not want to hear it, but he purposely deceived me, and many others!"

"I shall not argue with you, Miss Bennet. But George has been at my side since I was a child! When I was sad or alone, when my brother was away at school, George was always there for me and my father."

"I know that...but some of your recollections are different from reality. As fond as you are of Mr Wickham, you cannot marry a man for affectionate childhood memories. You should first know the full truth that your brother concealed from you in order to protect you from more grief."

"What truth, Miss Bennet? About the difference in our situations? In consequence? I am a gentleman's daughter, George has been brought up as a gentleman, my own father saw to that. I know George does not have a career yet, but he would have if my brother gave him the living promised by my father. I do not blame my brother, I am sure he had good reasons to refuse it, but I cannot blame George either."

"Miss Darcy, let us sit. It is not for me to reveal such important details, but I may not have another opportunity. And you may discuss it later with your brother or ask for more proof and details. Are you aware that your brother paid Mr Wickham three thousand pounds in lieu of the living when he changed his mind about taking orders? And in spite of that, he repeatedly asked for more money? Do you know how much your brother has paid Mr Wickham since your father's passing?"

The revelation made Miss Darcy even paler, and she looked at Elizabeth with her lips parted, but the words failed to come out.

"That is a falsehood, it cannot be true," the girl finally whispered.

"Unfortunately, it is true. You know your brother would not lie about such things. I would suggest you ask your cousin, the colonel, who I understand is your guardian along with your brother. He is aware of all the transactions and can corroborate your brother's story."

Miss Darcy only shook her head in denial, and Elizabeth watched the girl with her heart aching.

"How do you know all this?" she eventually asked.

"I know because I trusted and believed Mr Wickham too. When we first met, he told me many malicious things about Mr Darcy, and I never doubted him. I thought very ill of your brother and even confronted him in a horrible fight. Perhaps hoping to clear his name and honour, your brother told me of their dealings."

"There is nothing malicious about my brother — he is the best of men. But he is always so proper, so dutiful, so flawless in his behaviour and successful in every endeavour. George is nowhere near as perfect, and my brother always demanded and expected too much from him. But I do love George, and I am sure he will be a good husband to me. And our father loved him. Papa would have heartily approved of me marrying him. He told me as much."

Elizabeth shook her head in doubt. "Yes, Mr Darcy told me that you wrote that. But may I ask when? When did your father mention to you that he would approve of you marrying Mr Wickham? Do you remember the time or the place or the situation when he told you that?"

Miss Darcy looked disoriented. "I am not quite sure...I was very young, and I hardly remember."

"Precisely. Could it be that you do not really remember such a statement *at all*, but Mr Wickham mentioned it to you, persuaded you that it was your own memory, even manipulated you to force your decision?"

"I...I do not think he...I do not know..."

"And, my dear Miss Darcy, even if your father had ever thought of your marriage, would he approve of it now, when you are still so young, when Mr Wickham has no career, no steady income, no means to take care of a wife and a family? Or did your father actually imagine that Mr Wickham would become a successful, hardworking, honourable man, striving for improvement, making good of the opportunities and education of a gentleman your father provided him with, waiting for a few more years and making sure he may support you properly when and if he marries you? After you have had time to know him better as a young woman, and with your brother's and guardian's approval?"

The interrogation disconcerted Miss Darcy, and as soft and warm as Elizabeth's voice was, her questions were as sharp and painful as arrows piercing the young girl's last defence. Tears moistened her eyes.

Elizabeth felt bad for being the bearer of such cruel revelations, but she knew she had to make the most of the time she had alone with Darcy's sister.

"Miss Darcy, your remembrance of a happy past where Mr Wickham had been close to you and your father, offering support and company...how was that possible when you yourself said that your father saw to it that he had a gentleman's education? He is your brother's age...should he not have been at school at the same time? Would your brother not have seen him in circumstances in which he was more unguarded? They were friends before, were they not? And if he was at Pemberley, have you never asked yourself why? Maybe his deportment was not that of Mr Darcy of Pemberley's godson? Or maybe he had been expelled? Therefore, that could be why he never actually finished his education?"

Seeing the girl become more and more troubled, Elizabeth searched her face, and when she caught her eye for few seconds, said, "Mr Wickham plans to live off your dowry once you are married, am I right? Have you given him any money already? I am sure you have. What explanation did he give you when he asked for it? Are his habits too expensive for a militia lieutenant's pay? And how was it possible for him to leave his regiment? We are at war. Will he be charged with treason?"

"I...I do not know...I have never thought of this...I have never asked..."

Seeing the young girl white as a sheet and at the edge of losing all composure, Elizabeth approached her slowly as she would a frightened kitten and took her hands in both of her own, speaking earnestly.

"I can see I am causing you pain. Forgive me, but I took the liberty of speaking to you as I would to my own sister, although I know I do not have the right to do so. I do not expect you to care about my words, nor to take my advice in earnest. But I beg you to speak to your brother, to ask him all those questions and to ask yourself what your father would think of this situation..."

"Even if I...it is too late now..."

"Not at all. May I ask where Mr Wickham is now?"

"He left to meet a friend. He has met many friends since we left Pemberley... He said he would return before midnight."

"Before midnight? But that is still hours from now! So he left you alone here? At this inn? In a locked room, without any refreshment?"

"He had to. He has some business to attend to..."

"Will you not come with me and wait for your brother at the inn where we are staying? We can leave Mr Wickham a note, and tomorrow you may talk again, all together, explain your feelings to your brother and decide what is best—"

"I cannot come with you, Miss Bennet."

"And I shall not leave you alone," Elizabeth said resolutely. "I shall stay here until your brother finds us. He will, eventually, you know that. He is looking for you at every inn and boarding house in the town, and he is determined and thorough, you know he is. Tom, your brother's coachman, is downstairs too."

"Miss Bennet, you do not understand. I have no other choice now. I left with George by design, I agreed to elope with him. If I returned home without being married, the scandal would ruin our name forever. I would rather keep my word than pollute both the Darcy and Fitzwilliam names. The scandal would ruin everybody's lives," Miss Darcy whispered, her eyes on the ground.

"I see... May I be so bold as to assume that Mr Wickham told you that, too? Just as he convinced you that your father would approve of your marriage, he made you fear the scandal so you could not change your mind. Am I wrong?"

Miss Darcy's answer was prevented and their discussion interrupted by a din of voices and the loud sound of an altercation, and suddenly Wickham burst into the room with Tom following him closely through the door, both men red-faced and agitated.

Chapter 10

"What the bloody hell are you doing here, Miss Bennet? And that bloody servant dared to stop me! What is happening here? Georgiana, what is the meaning of this? Why did you open the bloody door?"

As enraged as Wickham was and as much as he swore and bellowed while he stepped further into the room and towards Georgiana — whose panic was now complete and who seemed to shrink and want to disappear — Elizabeth suddenly calmed herself, and her spirit, determination, and strength rose in the face of such an attempt at intimidation.

"Mr Wickham! I might ask what *you* are doing here. I was all astonishment to hear you had eloped with Miss Darcy when I expected you to propose to Mary King only a month ago! We all waited for the news of your engagement to Mary after you started to pursue her. If I remember correctly, it was soon after she inherited the sum of ten thousand pounds."

Elizabeth's boldness petrified Miss Darcy but absolutely shocked Wickham, who blinked and swallowed repeatedly, trying to reply.

"Miss Bennet, you should leave before you make an even greater fool of yourself. I have not yet told Georgiana that you were absolutely smitten with me and hoped for more attention from me, which I refused to give. Now you are emboldened by jealousy and resentment and have come here to ruin our happiness."

Again, Miss Darcy was the one hurt and suffering the most. With the same calm and a broader smile on her face, Elizabeth responded, "Are you trying to offend and shame me by taunting me with the friendship I showed you, Mr Wickham? Do not bother to do so, I am already disgusted with myself and mortified by my stupidity in trusting you! Yes, I favoured you for a while. That is why I believed your spiteful gossip about Mr Darcy as well as about Miss Darcy! You do remember how ill you spoke of her too, I hope?"

Never expecting such a riposte, Wickham's audacity deflated, and he was again lost for words.

"This is not...I have not..."

"Of course it is, and you have, Mr Wickham! You seemed charmed by my company too, but that was prior to finding out about Mary King's inheritance. You even mentioned that, had it not been for Mr Darcy leaving you without the means to support yourself... But you know too well what I mean."

"I do not know what you mean, and I find this discussion ridiculous! You should leave immediately! You should not have come here in the first place, you have nothing to do with either me or Georgiana!"

"But I do have everything to do with both of you!" Darcy's voice thundered from the door, and his tall, impressive presence filled the room. Behind him was Mr Gardiner, Tom, and John, all three of them remaining outside the room.

Darcy stepped forward, and after assuring himself with a glance that Elizabeth was unharmed, he stopped inches from Georgiana.

"Dearest, do not be afraid. I am not here to force you in any way. I wish nothing else but to know you are unhurt. Nothing is more important to me than to know you are happy and content."

"Brother, I am not afraid of you…but I made a decision which will affect our lives and our families regardless. I must keep my word and act so as not to cause even more harm."

"No, no! I beg you not to make a mistake that will ruin your life! Trust me, I can fix anything. I can remedy any wrong! But knowing you are unhappy would never allow me to be happy either. And knowing you are suffering, I would… No, this does not bear contemplating!"

"Come now, Darcy, this is rather pathetic! All this drama you are trying to paint! We shall marry tomorrow and shall all be happy! I have always been fond of Georgiana, and I would not want a scandal to ruin her reputation! Think of what Lady Catherine would say. Or the earl? Surely you cannot expect her to make a good marriage after that! You will ruin her life with your foolishness and the undeserved grudge you hold against me! You and Miss Bennet here. By the way, it is strange how Miss Bennet used to despise you and suddenly she is your best friend! Pemberley has such an impact on women!" he concluded sarcastically.

Darcy's jaw tightened and his fists clenched, turning his knuckles white. "Wickham, shut up! Do not tempt me to act as I should have years ago. Do not force me to remove that grin from your face! You have the insolence to threaten us with a scandal? Would you spread gossip about her as you did with me? As a sign of gratitude for your godfather's generosity and affection for his daughter?"

"Brother, please..." Miss Darcy begged, looking desperately from one man to the other. "I am sure George would not..."

"He would, my dear! And he will!" Darcy replied, so angrily that the girl took a step back. "He would do anything for his personal gain or interest, regardless of who might be hurt!"

"George?" the girl turned to him, trembling with distress.

"Georgiana, we made a plan together, and we should respect it. If we do, all will be well." He tried to soften his voice for her sake but failed, and the menacing implications were not missed. "If not, I shall be hurt, and I cannot be held responsible for my actions!"

With Miss Darcy almost out of strength, with Darcy barely controlling his hot fury, and with Wickham wearing another self-confident grin, Elizabeth interjected coldly, "I am afraid this is all a big misunderstanding, and I would be happy to clarify it, if you will allow me? My uncle Gardiner had some business here in the North, and Mr Darcy was so kind as to assist him. Miss Darcy and I accompanied them, as neither of us had seen this part of the country, and we both wanted to strengthen our friendship after our recent acquaintance at Pemberley. On our journey, we unexpectedly met Mr Wickham, who is known to all of us and who is probably looking for a new commission here in the North—"

Her unexpected words seemed to make no sense and the confusion was universal.

"What?" Wickham interrupted, but Elizabeth continued with equal calmness.

"Yes...I am reasonably sure that the events of the last few days have provided you with enough money to purchase a new commission, and we wish you good luck with your endeavour. In the meantime, my uncle has concluded his affairs, so tomorrow we will all return to Pemberley. All four of us! Until then, Miss Darcy and I shall bid you goodbye and return to our inn, as we are very tired. John and Tom will, of course, escort us. You gentlemen may stay longer and conclude your conversation."

As everyone in the room started to understand Elizabeth's story's larger meaning, they each contemplated the outcome, so when she finished speaking, silence enveloped the room for a few minutes.

"You have lost your mind, Miss Bennet! Nobody will believe such a fabrication! You cannot avoid the scandal this way!"

Darcy was ready to react to the offence by force, but Elizabeth continued.

"Indeed? You plan then to contradict me and tell people another story? What would that be? That you planned to elope with Miss Darcy, a young heiress of sixteen years of age who has been like a little sister to you, after you have already tried to elope twice before, with other young ladies, whose fathers were close to shooting you?"

Silent, seethingly angry but powerless, seeing his carefully laid plans crumble, defeated with his own weapons, Wickham's face expressed a mixture of feelings, with fear more prominent now among them.

With tears rolling down her face, Miss Darcy looked at Wickham without him returning the glance. Then the girl turned to Darcy, whispering, "Brother, are you certain I can change my mind? Can I return home?"

His expression softened and brightened in an instant. "I am not just certain, my dear. It is the answer to all my prayers and hopes."

The girl nodded, stood tall, then gathered her strength to bid her goodbye, as though she was leaving a drawing room after a call.

"Miss Bennet is right. I find I am very tired. I would rather return with her to the inn. After all, tomorrow we shall travel back home."

Elizabeth gently took the girl's hand. It was cold and weak and trembled slightly, but Elizabeth supported and guided her out the room. In the hall, Mr Gardiner, Tom, and John had been watching silently. After they exited, Mr Gardiner stepped inside.

Before the door closed behind him, Elizabeth caught a glimpse of Darcy's gaze full of emotion following her. Gratitude, admiration, and some other feelings made his stare even darker and deeper — yet so warm and tender.

Chapter 11

Georgiana Darcy was sitting gingerly on the edge of her bed, her eyes to the floor, her hands clasped in her lap, her bonnet lying at her side.

Facing her, on a chair placed a short distance away, Elizabeth waited, struggling to curb her own impatience. Darcy and her uncle had not returned yet, and she wondered how their interaction with Wickham was proceeding.

On the table was a tray full of small covered dishes containing a variety of food, all untouched.

"I have no words to apologise...I feel like I want to die or at least to disappear...of shame...and pain..." Miss Darcy whispered.

"I can imagine how you must feel, Miss Darcy. But you will not die. Besides, we wish you in good health now and in good spirits sometime soon. Especially your brother."

"Would you not call me Georgiana, please?" she asked in a weak voice.

"It would be my pleasure. But only if you call me Elizabeth."

"I am sorry for all the trouble I have caused you, Elizabeth...I fear to imagine what you think of me. And my poor brother...how can he ever forgive me?"

"Miss D...Georgiana, for my part, I think you have made an imprudent mistake, as many young ladies are wont to do, as my younger sister has done too many times, not to mention myself! I have been plagued by the shame of my own errors too many times in the last few months, but believe me when I tell you that, eventually, the agony becomes bearable."

"I doubt your errors compare to mine, Elizabeth. My mistake is much worse, more mortifying, as it was done by design and long planned. I have been a ninny for a very long time..."

"Yes, you have," Elizabeth agreed, and the girl stared at her, surprised.

"Georgiana, you are too clever and too well-educated a young woman for me to even attempt to say that your misadventure was not dangerous and life-changing in many ways. But it has happened to many other women before and will surely happen again in the future. Your brother will forgive and forget long before you will, I am sure. He wished nothing but to know you were safe and healthy."

"*You* are a clever and educated woman, Elizabeth. You would never have been fooled by such a man. You would never have risked your family's name or exposed them to shame and ruin."

"Oh, my dear girl, you are so very sweet and generous. You resemble my sister Jane so much, and just like her, you are partial to me and not correct at all. I am much older than you, and I thought myself clever, and still I did allow myself to be fooled, by none other than the same Mr Wickham. Should you wish it, I shall tell you all the details of my own foolishness one day."

"Oh…Elizabeth, is it true that he spoke ill of me? And my brother?"

"Yes," Elizabeth replied hesitantly. "To be truthful, of you he only said that you were very proud and unpleasant in manners, 'just like your brother'. What bothered me the most was that he specifically informed me that he had not seen you in a few years — which is a clear sign of his deceptive and devious plans."

Georgiana lowered her eyes again dejectedly and nodded.

"What will happen now?" she asked. "Oh, I did not take my trunk from there, I have nothing with me to wear, no clothes at all…" She spoke with much difficulty, her voice almost inaudible, strangled by tears.

Elizabeth moved closer to her and took her hands.

"You really should not worry yourself with that. I shall find something from my own trunk for you for tonight, even though you are taller than me, and tomorrow we may purchase more clothes for the journey back. It will give you something else to think about. All will be well, I promise, Georgiana. I know everything looks gloomy now, and I can only imagine how much pain is in your heart and how despondent you feel…"

"I am more troubled by Fitzwilliam's pain than mine. I am such a bother to him. He must be hurt and disappointed…and he has every reason to resent me—"

"Resent you? Dearest, how can you even say that? I have rarely seen a brother so affectionate, so devoted to his sister! He speaks about you with so much admiration and pride! There is no other subject on which he is more eloquent. I am sure he would do anything for you!"

"I know, he is the best brother in the world. But he was already upset with me when..." The girl paused and looked at Elizabeth, indecision clear in her eyes. "You would despise me too if you knew...it was not the first time when...last summer I tried to elope with George for the first time, but I confessed the plan to my brother just before..."

Elizabeth hesitated a moment, wondering how to react. With no time for much consideration, she decided to choose honesty.

"I knew that. Mr Darcy told me in the strictest confidence. Nobody else knows..."

"Oh...you knew? Oh...so...I am sure you wonder how it could happen again...how could I have been such a goose, a ridiculous silly goose twice..."

Again, Elizabeth squeezed her hands and replied sincerely.

"I do wonder. But I am sure Wickham must have persuaded you in some way. It was not difficult for him to succeed since you knew little of his many flaws of character."

"I can hardly believe what I heard earlier. I knew he was not flawless. Even he, himself, admitted his failings and his lack of ambition. He said he would change for me, once we were married..." Tears overwhelmed her, and she sobbed while Elizabeth embraced her.

"Georgiana, you may not answer if you do not wish to, but I must enquire. When did you speak about all this with Wickham? How? I understood from your brother that all connection with Wickham was to be severed after last summer..."

"I saw George in London last autumn. My brother was at Netherfield then, visiting Mr Bingley. I met him by chance one day when I was walking in Hyde Park...and then I received a letter from him..."

"A letter? How did Mrs Annesley allow it?"

Georgiana hesitated again, her hands rising to cover her face. "He signed it as Lady Anna Bell...he called me that when I was a child. Belle Anna, which means beautiful Anna. Only the two of us ever knew or used that name, so I recognised the letter. I know I should not have read it, but I did..."

Elizabeth immediately understood that Wickham had taken advantage of knowing precisely where Darcy was, and understanding that Georgiana was alone in London, attempted to approach his victim. She was horrified by such audacity. It also dawned on her that this had probably happened during the Netherfield ball — Wickham's sudden business causing his absence from the ball by 'obliging him to go to town' as his friend Mr Denny pronounced — and she recalled how at almost the same time she was attacking Darcy on the blackguard's behalf.

"Then"— Georgiana's feeble voice brought Elizabeth back from memories of her own silliness— "Fitzwilliam returned from Hertfordshire, and he was simply not himself. He spent more time in his library. He was very kind to me, but I felt he was somewhat different. And then he went to Kent, to visit Aunt Catherine, and George happened to be in town at the same time."

"Indeed! How convenient," Elizabeth slipped the remark, rolling her eyes.

"And when Fitzwilliam returned from Kent, everything changed...he was changed...I have never seen him like that. He barely spoke to me at all...or to anyone. He refused calls, he would not go to his club. He would rarely see our family. I am sure he was upset with me. I did not even know why... He could not have found out about me meeting George or about his letter. He avoided my company. He barely left his library at all...I found him drinking alone several times, other times he slept there, at the desk and when I asked, he claimed all was well...so...”

Every word broke Elizabeth's heart a bit more, and the unexpected account delivered by so genuine a witness placed a block of ice in her stomach. Words failed her, so she listened in silence, hoping the girl would not notice how ill she felt. While Georgiana was completely unsuspecting of the effect her report was having and was oblivious to the reason, Elizabeth could easily deduce the cause for Darcy's altered behaviour. She had assumed that her rejection had affected him, but the dark picture drawn by the girl's shaky confession grasped her by the throat.

“Did Wickham know?” she managed to ask.

“Yes, I wrote to him.”

“At his regiment?”

“Yes...I know it was unconscionable of me, foolish, but I was desperate! And he always listened to me and understood me. He replied that perhaps Fitzwilliam would rather live by himself, like any young man. He said that perhaps Fitzwilliam had not married yet because he had to take care of me...that perhaps it would be better to move into my own townhouse, that I should ask Fitzwilliam again that an establishment be made for me. And so it began...I did not move from Darcy House, but we wrote a few times, and one day, when I was back at Pemberley and visiting Mrs Skinner, I met him there, in the park. I did not think to ask how it came about that he was there. I was so surprised. Now, I realise he came undoubtedly by design. He said he loved me and always would and that my brother would eventually accept our marriage and would be relieved of the burden of being my guardian...and that he would work hard to build a career and to convince Fitzwilliam he was a good husband to me. He said nobody would understand me better than him...”

It was the longest string of words that Elizabeth had ever

heard from Georgiana. The long tirade seemed to both tire her and relieve her of a great weight from her chest. The more she spoke, the easier the words came out, and the tears flowed freely like the dam of her suffering was suddenly released. Sitting by her side and trying to comfort her, Elizabeth shared the girl's grief and took it upon herself, burdened by her own guilt and remorse.

"Now I know he played me ill. Despite appearances, I am not a complete simpleton, I did become alarmed the moment I left Pemberley. But he calmed me, assured me all would be well. I wished to believe and to trust him, more than I did... But then, it was too late to return. I dreaded to imagine how Miss Bingley and Mrs Hurst would have reacted and what Lady Catherine would say. Or Aunt Matlock. I would rather die than face their disapproval and contempt. And now that I am to return home, if Fitzwilliam allows me, I shall remain at Pemberley for the rest of my days."

Trying to think of only Georgiana's pain, Elizabeth embraced her tighter, stroking her hair.

"I hope none of your fears are justified. Only Mr Bingley knows the truth, and we may depend on his secrecy. He resolved to take his family back to London urgently. His sisters were told you were in your room, but you had taken suddenly ill, probably catching something contagious from the tenant family you were visiting. Mrs Annesley also knows since she was the one who found your note and brought it to your brother. And Mrs Reynolds and my aunt were also told of the secret, but I do not doubt their discretion. When we return, we may tell everyone the story about our visit to the North. There might be some raised brows, perhaps rumours and discreet enquiries. Our claims might be doubted, but who would dare contradict it openly?"

Georgiana's blue eyes widened in astonishment. They

were still glistening with tears hanging on her lashes, but she had calmed enough to begin to comprehend the new information.

"You have thought of everything... You knew I would not marry George?"

"We hoped — your brother hoped you would not, regardless of what happened. He already told you he would do anything and fix everything for you."

"He did. I was so horribly ungrateful for doubting him and hiding things from him and going completely against his advice and wishes! I allowed myself to be convinced. I should have known better...what a fool I have been. And now, once again, my brother will have to sort out my predicament and struggle with the consequences."

"All is well now. You must eat something and then try to rest. And tomorrow we will discuss what more is to be done."

"Do you think Fitzwilliam will hurt George?" Georgiana blurted out suddenly, brow furrowed and eyes clouding again.

Elizabeth forced herself to be calm, counted to three, and spoke only when certain her voice was also steadier, "I hope Wickham will have the prudence to act and speak in such a manner as to avoid being hurt! I am sure it will depend on him entirely."

"But what will happen to him now? He has left his regiment...he has no other way of living..."

"His scheme will surely bring him many problems, for which he is the only person responsible. And I am certain he has some money to survive from what you gave him, has he not? May I ask how much it was?"

Georgiana shook her head. "Not too much...I believe I had five hundred pounds...but I am not sure if he still has it. I believe he played cards. He met friends at every inn we stayed at. He was gone most nights, and I am not sure whether he won or lost."

Elizabeth gasped, shocked and outraged at hearing such a sum, then became angry.

"Not too much? My dear, I find myself quite disinclined to feel indulgent right now. You gave him a small fortune and you still worry about how he will live. Do you truly understand just how much money you wasted on him? How did you even come by such an amount? Did he ask for it? This is too much. He has been given so much from each of the Darcys, and he has wasted everything carelessly in a short time! And now he has tried to waste your life too! I hope he will pay for all his faults and finally learn his lesson!"

"Oh! You must not worry I have stolen from my brother! It was from my allowance. Fitzwilliam is so generous, aside from what my father already left me, and I do not need that much, so in time, I...George did not exactly ask, but he mentioned he had no more pay from the regiment and that the journey north was expensive, so I..."

Georgiana coloured and was on the brink of tears anew. She lowered her eyes and almost inaudibly continued.

"I know what you are thinking. I understand and I am thinking it also. But to me, he was very kind...and patient. He did not even attempt to...you know... He barely kissed my hand a few times...he never... If he had, I would never dare face my brother again. And despite taking advantage, I still believe George cares about me..."

Georgiana's confession dissipated Elizabeth's greatest worry, something she had struggled to enquire about but had not found the courage or opportunity to do so, the relief she felt making her almost forget her exasperation and her desire to shake the girl. Wickham had behaved like a gentleman in one way at least, as had rarely been the case in his life. Not even a profligate such as he dared to impose himself or force the daughter of his godfather in any manner, a girl who had grown up from infancy before his eyes.

"I am sure he cares about you, my dear. How could he not? But he abused your trust and affection for easy gains. That is the truth. He might have a good heart, as you said, but his actions and his character are deficient. He is clever enough and well educated by the generosity of your father, but he chose a dishonourable way to use his qualities!"

"You are right of course…and I would like to take your advice now and rest a little."

While the girl took off her spencer and Elizabeth busied herself searching in her trunk for something for Georgiana to wear to bed, the young girl suddenly asked, "Elizabeth, may I ask…why are *you* here? I am grateful for your presence, do not think otherwise. But why did you take all this trouble? My brother told me about your past arguments and how rudely he behaved at the beginning of your acquaintance. How did it happen that he confessed everything to you? And why did you travel with him all this way, to find me?"

Elizabeth felt her cheeks flushing, while she pondered how to reply.

"I was with your brother in the library when Mrs Annesley came with your note. He read your letter and told me about its contents since I was there. He was so shocked and devastated, the grief clouded his reason, and we feared he might act precipitously and imprudently and put himself in danger. I spoke to my uncle… Besides, I felt you may need a female friend to speak to, especially since I was no stranger to Wickham's schemes and deceptions. I hope you do not mind."

"I am happy you came, Elizabeth. I could not believe how

brave you were in confronting George! I could have never...I have never met any lady like you. Indeed, I am glad you came," the girl repeated.

"I am glad you are glad, my dear," Elizabeth attempted to joke. "Now please keep me company, we must eat a little — I confess I am also very thirsty — and then you may rest. I shall be in the other room."

"Very well...Elizabeth, are you and my brother still arguing? Are you still displeased with his behaviour?"

"Not as much as in the past," Elizabeth replied, trying a light jocular tone to conceal her uneasiness. "I must claim a fair share of blame in our past misunderstandings. His manners were not always amiable, but neither were mine. He was proud and disdainful, I was prejudiced and imprudent. I listened to and trusted Wickham's falsehoods, which affected my opinion of Mr Darcy even more. He made some errors, but he has remedied most of them, for which I am grateful to him."

"I am relieved to hear that. He is truly the best of men."

"I know that. Once I discovered his true character, I could not but admire it and improve my opinion of him."

"He thinks very highly of you. I have never heard him speak so admiringly, so fondly of another lady. He was so very happy that you came to Pemberley, Elizabeth. It was a fortunate occurrence."

"A fortunate occurrence, indeed," Elizabeth admitted, sounding calmer than she really was.

Half an hour later, after a cup of tea, Georgiana finally fell asleep, but not before she asked several times why Darcy and Mr Gardiner had been delayed so long.

Despite her finding several good explanations for Georgiana's sake, Elizabeth wondered the same, and she prayed there had not been an escalation of violence between the men.

Knowing she would never be able to sleep, both because of her long and emotional conversation with Georgiana and her impatience to hear news, she installed herself on the windowsill. As her room had windows looking out onto the street, she stared outside into the darkness for a while, until she finally recognised the two long-awaited riders. Minutes later, Mr Gardiner knocked on her door, and she opened it in haste.

"Lizzy, all is well. We spoke to Mr Wickham and will discuss it more tomorrow. I am too tired now. I shall eat something in my room and sleep — at last. You should do the same. I shall see you tomorrow morning."

"Good night, Uncle," she said, closing the door slowly but remaining near it. After a few moments, she opened it a crack, hoping, waiting to see Darcy passing towards his own room, until he appeared eventually.

"Mr Darcy?" she called him in a whisper.

"Miss Bennet…I had hoped to find you still awake. How are you? How is Georgiana?"

His countenance was etched with worry, and he was pale, his brows knitted and with dark circles around his eyes.

"She is asleep. I believe she is reasonably well. We talked for a long time…"

They were in the doorway, and she opened it a little more.

"Would you not come inside for a moment? We still have some food that is untouched. I imagine you are hungry…"

He hesitated briefly, looking behind him at the empty hall, and she thought he would refuse again, like the night before, berating herself for making the enquiry.

"I would like that very much…that is if it does not disturb

you. It is very late and..."

"I know it is very late and that I should not ask you, but I am doing it, nevertheless. I have not eaten much either, and I would like your company," she replied, aware of her unseemly boldness.

He smiled a bit, tiredly, but was clearly pleased. "I am starving, in fact. For food and for good company," he replied with more honesty than decorum. But it was neither the time nor the place to worry about society's rules too much.

He entered swiftly, and she closed the door behind him, finding themselves alone in the small sitting room, after midnight, at the end of a day which had certainly affected their lives.

Chapter 12

They sat opposite each other at the table in the barely lit room, Georgiana sleeping a few feet away in the next chamber, both slightly embarrassed but too exhausted to be concerned.

"I shall only stay for a moment. I ought not to be here, and I do not want to trouble you for long. Has Georgiana been asleep for some time? I imagine she was exhausted."

"No, she has not been asleep for long. She needed some time to comprehend all that had happened, to gather a little calm and tranquillity. You look exhausted too, Mr Darcy. You should rest."

"So do you. Before anything else, I must tell you that I have never met a woman more obstinate and persistent," he said in earnest. "Nor have I ever felt so much admiration or gratitude for anyone else, Miss Bennet," he continued, while her heart was racing.

"Is that a compliment or a criticism, Mr Darcy?" she said with a trace of teasing in her voice, trying as was her habit to cover her emotions with a joke.

"Both, Miss Bennet. When I arrived at the inn...actually, I had met Mr Gardiner earlier, after we had both checked as many inns and guesthouses as we could, and we knew there were only two more places at which to enquire. I was stunned to see Tom there, and when he told me you were upstairs, fighting with Wickham, my anger just flared up. I lost my temper, and I ran to the room. I must confess I feared the worst. Then I heard you arguing with Wickham, your words penetrating my rage, and the fright turned into admiration."

His praise, spoken in his earnest and honest voice, and his words, less restrained than in other circumstances, unguarded, matching the serious expression on his face, caused her pleasant nervousness and thrills.

"I confess I was so angry and appalled by Wickham's insolence that I barely remember what I said," she admitted. "I had arrived there some moments earlier and spent the time talking to Georgiana, and when he appeared...upon my word, I was ready to actually fight with him."

"I believe you would have," he smiled. "I dare say courage and a little anger suits you well, Miss Bennet. I am more inclined to appreciate it when it is not directed at me."

His small smile remained, and the slightly upturned corners of his lips pressed together softened his features. But it was his eyes, his gaze, that made her shiver.

"I am glad you are in better spirits now and willing to tease, Mr Darcy. But you should eat — you are yet to touch anything on the trays, and you said you were starving," she replied, hoping the thrills would not affect her voice too.

"I shall eat. Perhaps later on, in my room, after a drink. For now, I am satisfied with the company. But please, you may eat if you wish."

"The company is enough for me too, for now..." she

admitted shyly.

A little pause followed, allowing the voices from outside to enter through the window.

"Shall we not return home tomorrow?" Instantly realising what she had said, she felt her face burning. "I mean to Pemberley? My uncle said you still have unfinished business with Mr Wickham?"

"Yes...I must be certain I have found the best way to deal with him, to silence any rumours and avoid unforeseen problems."

"Georgiana was afraid you might hurt him."

"It is a wonder I did not. I congratulate myself on my excellent self-control. He is a miserable human being, I am sorry to say."

"Do not be sorry. He is even worse than that. He designed and planned the entire scheme carefully, taking advantage of Georgiana's kindness and credulity. There is something Georgiana told me..." She started to speak, then stopped, uncertain whether it was wise to proceed.

"Yes?" he gently encouraged her, curious but disquieted, and she was too tired to find excuses to change the subject.

"Georgiana noticed that you were somewhat preoccupied and even out of spirits when you returned from Hertfordshire, then even worse when you returned from Kent...She truly believed you were upset with her, disappointed with her after last year's troubles...and that it would be better for you if she had her own life. She wrote to Wickham, and he abused her trust, planning how to use her torment for his own benefit."

The hurt and sadness clouded his expression again, and his eyebrows furrowed.

"But how? Why would she think that? I was never upset or disappointed with her, I thought I had been clear on that matter! And Wickham, the bloody useless dastard! In the end, I was right — I am indeed to blame, it was all my fault!" he concluded, shaking his head.

She stretched her hands over the small table and grasped his.

"It was not your fault! Let us not speak of it tonight. All is well now."

He was surprised by her gesture for an instant and searched her eyes, then his hands slowly turned, allowing hers to rest in his palms.

"We should rest and think more clearly tomorrow. Know that there are no other urgent reasons for distress now. Georgiana told me that...she had not...he did not...they were not..." She swallowed, blushing furiously at having to speak about this but determined he would not suffer from imagining things were any worse. "It seems there will be no consequences of this elopement. She said Wickham behaved in a very gentlemanlike manner, and nothing improper happened..."

Her cheeks were burning at her audacity in addressing such a subject to him in the middle of the night.

He nodded, slightly tightening his hands around hers, and replied, "Thank you for telling me. He also told me as much, but I am glad I have not only his word on this matter. It is a comfort to know she is unharmed and will not have to suffer more consequences. I am lost as to how to do...it pains me to realise how little I understand my sister and how poorly I have shown her my affection."

"It was only a deep and painful misunderstanding. *We* both know too well the reason for your low spirits, at least after Kent. I could blame myself too. But Mr Darcy, let us stop this unnecessary torment. We cannot change it now, and it has been enough for today. Let us get some rest, what say you?"

"You are correct, of course. Tomorrow, we have another difficult day ahead, then several more days on the road. I shall settle things with Wickham tomorrow — Mr Gardiner will be my witness."

"I am sure you will fix everything, and solve any problems," Elizabeth smiled. "Everyone says as much about you, and now I can attest to it myself."

She was trying to lighten his mood, but he tightened his grip on her hands again, and his thumbs gently brushed over her knuckles.

"I was able to solve everything because you were by my side, Miss Bennet. I have you to support me, to guard me, to temper me, to show me the direction when I missed it. I have never felt so complete, so confident, so trusting as I am in your presence. I was so fortunate to have you…here, with me, I mean. And so was Georgiana. Your absence will be painful to bear…" he confessed in a voice turned suddenly throatier and hesitant.

The emotions made her speak with difficulty, breathe with difficulty, and all her senses gathered at that spot where his hands were clasping hers and his fingers were caressing hers.

"Mr Darcy, I am not going anywhere, sir. At least not yet. I am glad I could be of help. And I am fortunate to be here, too. With you, for you and Georgiana…"

He lifted their joined hands to his lips, and in silence, slowly, almost reverently, he placed a kiss on each of them. She sighed but did not withdraw. Then, he turned her hands, and his lips rested on the interior of her wrists for another moment. Brief, gentle, sweet, as soft as the summer breeze.

And then, his eyes rose and met hers again. "It is very late.

I should leave you to rest now. Good night, Miss Bennet."

"Good night, Mr Darcy," she whispered as he gently released her hands and left the room, with one last long, serious glance at her.

As the door closed, her fingers already missed his caresses, and the delicate skin where he had placed his lips tingled. Blushing, amazed at what she was about to do but thrilled at the almost forbidden sensation, she slowly touched her own lips to where his had been, and understood how right he was: to her, his absence was already painful to bear.

Chapter 13

Before she could allow herself to rest though, Elizabeth went to check on Georgiana. The girl was sleeping, but she woke up with a start at her entrance. Elizabeth put her at ease, explaining that Darcy and her uncle had returned to the inn to get some sleep, that they were still in the process of settling things with Wickham and would continue on the morrow, but they all were well and unharmed. It took some time until both of them finally went to sleep. Elizabeth's natural distress after such a day was amplified by her feelings for Darcy and their most recent interlude, the delight of the almost illicit nearness they had shared and the newness of the sensations she had felt at his touch. She felt that she had reasons to hope but also to have concerns, worrying she might have assumed too much from his actions or words.

The dawn finally came and brought some peace and rest for Elizabeth. She overslept, and only Georgiana knocking on her door startled her awake.

"Come, come, please. I had not realised it was so late. I think I was more tired than I realised. I shall be but a moment," she apologised with some agitation looking for her garments.

"There is no reason to hurry, Elizabeth. You may sleep longer if you wish. Tom has just brought me my trunk. He said my brother and your uncle have already left to conclude the affairs. I assume he meant with George. Hopefully, all is well."

"I am sure they will reach an acceptable understanding. Although I have to say, any gesture of kindness on Mr Darcy's part is commendable and undeserved."

"I know, Miss B...Elizabeth...I wish the last months had never happened...I wish last year had never happened!"

The girl's dejection was plain, and her grief had obviously not been soothed overnight. Elizabeth tried to comfort her, inwardly thinking that she could not but heartily disagree with her wish. If the last year had never occurred, she might have been saved from much distress, but also prevented from the joy of meeting Darcy and all the overwhelming feelings — different over time, opposite even, but always powerful and impossible to ignore — that he had brought into her life.

Whilst waiting for the gentlemen to return, Elizabeth and Georgiana, with more appetite than the evening before, had a good breakfast in their room, then eventually prepared for the journey ahead and packed their belongings. It was expected they would leave as soon as the business with Wickham was completed, unless it was too late in the day.

Normally, Elizabeth would have used that time for another walk — this time with no other purpose than to enjoy the exercise — and to see a bit more of the town. However, Georgiana was less inclined and still apprehensive of any contact with strangers, so they remained inside, talking.

Around noon, they heard voices in the hall and a knock on the door. Mr Darcy entered, looking at both of them with some uneasiness.

"All is done. We can depart for home, if that is acceptable

to you, ladies."

"We can? And…George?" Georgiana asked timidly.

"We have reached an understanding. Considering our past relationship and the affection our father had for him, I promised to support him to find new employment. He decided he would like to join another regiment here, in the North. We wrote to Colonel Forster, at his regiment, and to Fitzwilliam, as well as to my solicitors in London. It will take a while to have everything arranged, so until then, Wickham will remain here. He has all his expenses paid at the inn for the next month, but it should not take that long."

"Oh…thank you, Brother," the girl whispered. "I am so happy you are helping him. This situation…I should be blamed for it, I started it, I encouraged it. I only hope he will find his way and his place after all."

"I hope the same, but I have little confidence. My dear, I know that you gave him some money. I told him he may keep it. I do not wish for another argument on this subject."

"Oh…thank you again, Brother! F-for the money…it was my pin money…I shall not ask for more, I promise!"

"Georgiana, you are entitled to use your allowance in any way you wish, and you will continue to receive it regularly. However, if one knows that he can easily make money without much trouble, one will never be induced to make any effort to secure an honourable living."

"Yes, I know…I have been blind and foolish. And very immature. I hope you will forgive me one day," she pleaded, her eyes to the floor from shame. Darcy stepped forward and embraced her gently, and she accepted the comfort for a little while.

"Forgive me. I only need a moment to refresh myself, then

I shall be ready to go," she said, hurrying into the room she had slept in.

Only then did Darcy meet Elizabeth's eyes. He saw in them the recognition of being again alone, in the same room as last night, and the memory of their hands joined together.

"So it all worked out rather well," she uttered. "I assume you demanded he remain here for a month. Did he consent to act like a gentleman and accept your requests and rein his own within reason, after all? He should have, considering he made another small fortune from you and Georgiana in only a few days."

"No, he did not," Darcy replied, moving near her so he could speak in a low voice. "He did not act like a gentleman, and neither did I. He is a despicable scoundrel. He blamed Georgiana for the elopement, he threatened me with the scandal, and he had the effrontery to tell me he had more debts to cover than Georgiana's 'paltry' allowance could afford. I shall not trouble you with it all. Suffice to say, he will have to stay in his room for a few days so his face can heal," he concluded, rubbing his right fist. Elizabeth did not miss the gesture.
"You hit him?" she enquired with disbelief.

"I did, and I am ashamed to admit that it gave me much pleasure and satisfaction. I acted like a savage, I know. Mr Gardiner was probably appalled since he witnessed the entire scene."

To his astonishment — would she ever cease to amaze him, he wondered absently — she smiled with mischief, and on an impulse, she took his right fist in her small hands, caressing his knuckles.

"I am sure my uncle felt equal satisfaction and pleasure watching you. I would have, had I been there. I hope you did not hurt your hand. You have suffered enough from Wickham."

Her voice — half teasing, half affectionate — and the silent expression in her eyes dissipated most of his anger and distress.

"If I did, it was well worth it only to feel your touch," he confessed, covering her hands with his left one. She blushed and allowed for several moments the stolen — yet so delightful — sensation of their entwined hands, then gently removed hers.

"We should leave, should we not?" she asked.

"Yes, it is time to return home," he replied, and her heart ached as she recollected that she would have to travel even further, to Hertfordshire, very soon. She could not call Pemberley her home, at least not yet.

∞∞∞

The first part of the return journey was mostly silent, and awkward, as Georgiana's distress and remorse was painful to watch. She sat on the cushion next to Elizabeth, looking outside, and rarely contributed to the conversation. She looked mortified, fighting her own thoughts, almost crushed under the shame of her actions, barely looking at her brother and even less so at Mr Gardiner.

The hurry was not as necessary on their way back, but they still travelled with as much haste as possible. They also spent three nights at inns, and each of them allowed Georgiana the opportunity to become closer to Elizabeth. As restrained as she was with her brother, she opened her heart to a friend who was old enough and wise enough to be trusted, but young enough to understand her.

Darcy found several opportunities to talk privately to Elizabeth; only short conversations, lasting just moments, mostly enquiries after each other's comfort and well-being, but the warmth of the thoughts behind the enquiries was fulfilling for both of them. The added countless moments — in the carriage, across the table while dining, before retiring for the night — when their gazes met and held, conveying so much, completed an as yet unspoken understanding, stronger with every hour, every mile of road covered.

However, these moments were bittersweet for Elizabeth, as she knew their arrival at Pemberley, although it would be the conclusion of a most disturbing situation, would also mean starting her preparations for returning to her family.

"From my calculations, we should arrive at Pemberley late in the evening. To avoid any unnecessary disruption, we should enter through the side door. I trust we shall find Mrs Gardiner at Pemberley too — Mr Gardiner wrote to her from Carlisle. We will have to talk to Mrs Annesley and Mrs Reynolds as soon as we alight and see what has been talked about, what the servants know, so we can adjust our story accordingly. We claimed Georgiana was ill, but surely the servants will know she has not been locked in her apartment for seven days and nights now."

"Brother, I am so sorry you have to lie for me. I know how much you abhor deceit. Mr Gardiner, Elizabeth, I deeply apologise..." Georgiana pleaded, affected by the new reminder.

"Miss Darcy, you have no reason to apologise to me, I assure you," Mr Gardiner tried warmly to comfort her. "I only pray we can leave all this behind and see you and Mr Darcy at peace again."

"Tonight, we shall be home. That is all that matters now," Darcy confirmed. "There will be peace and tranquillity at Pemberley since there will be nobody but us," he said, his glance conveying to Elizabeth that she, as well as her relatives, were part of that 'us'.

After more hours of travelling with barely any stops at all, pushed by the anticipation of reaching home, they entered Pemberley Park at dusk, immediately enveloped in the quietness and soothing familiarity of the charming surroundings.

Even the horses calmed their pace; only Elizabeth's heart was racing when the house came into sight. It was a serene summer night, with the sky lit by stars and a bright moon, mirrored in the lake — a picture of perfect enchanting beauty which Elizabeth observed tearfully, wondering for how long she would see it. She knew she could expect Darcy to speak up soon. He was not the sort of man to show her all that attention without having a serious design on her. To anyone's reasonable judgment, there were clear signs that he would express himself, that he would propose soon. However, she could not ignore the special circumstances in which those attentions were granted; the feeling of gratitude he had confessed so many times had certainly influenced his behaviour, as well as placated somewhat the recollection of her horrible rejection from only a few months ago.

Once returned to their daily lives, with no spectre of drama and scandal over their heads, with Darcy clearing his mind and putting his thoughts in order, would he find the strength to forgive and forget the offences and disappointment — and propose to her again?

"Miss Bennet? We are home," she heard the voice that gave her shivers. He was already out of the carriage, and so were her uncle and Georgiana. He stretched his hand out to her, and Elizabeth took it, then all walked together towards a smaller door she had never seen before, which allowed them to step into the comfort of Pemberley.

Georgiana hastened towards her apartment, and as she climbed the stairs, Mrs Annesley and Mrs Reynolds followed protectively. Elizabeth retired to her room too, a few doors away from the girl's, and upon entering, she heard her uncle and Darcy's voices behind her, down the hall.

Some of her luggage was still there, and she had the satisfying feeling of being home, just as Darcy had said. She leant back against the pillows and closed her eyes for a few moments, the bed reminding her how tired she was. She startled when she heard a knock at the door, and her heart pounded as she imagined it might be Darcy. Surprisingly, Mrs Gardiner entered, and she hurried to embrace Elizabeth.

"My dear aunt, I did not expect you to be here!"

"Your uncle wrote to me from Carlisle. He said that Mr Darcy suggested that I would not be comfortable enough at the inn in Lambton and should move to Pemberley with all our belongings. Tell me everything! How was your journey? Your uncle is with Mr Darcy in the library — I assume they are having a drink, maybe more than just one in your uncle's case — so I came to see you and hear all the details you can share."

Elizabeth narrated their adventures for Mrs Gardiner, and her aunt listened with concern and dismay.

"I cannot believe what a deceptive man that Mr Wickham is! I confess I did not suspect such a deceitful character when I met him last Christmas! I remember being worried that you might be smitten with him, despite the fact that neither of you had any security for the future. I believed it would have been dangerous for you to marry him, but only because of his situation in life, I did not doubt his character! How he misled us all!"

"Yes...and I cannot forgive myself for that. Although I have never been smitten with him, I did enjoy his company, and I never doubted his claims, nor did I see the impropriety of his confessions because I felt flattered by his attention and offended by Mr Darcy's past remarks and behaviour. Foolish, foolish girl I was!"

"You must forgive yourself, Lizzy. Mr Darcy certainly has. Oh, let me tell you that I have heard a lot of stories about him from Mrs Reynolds and other servants these past few days while I have been here. He really is the best master and landlord, at least that is what they all claim. And who knows him better or praises him more honestly than a faithful and intelligent servant? I have heard stories about Mr Wickham as well. He is known of course by the household. They had heard he had gone into the army, but they feared 'he had turned out very wild'! And I visited the Skinners. I accompanied Mrs Reynolds one day. They have recovered completely. Those three children are really sweet. Miss Darcy will be pleased to hear that, I am certain."

"Dear aunt, what do the servants know about Georgiana? What were they told?"

"Well, we kept to the story that she was ill. Mrs Annesley ate most of her meals in her room, and Mrs Reynolds kept her company. I did hear some rumours among the servants that Miss Darcy had not been seen for an entire week — but there are few who usually have reasons to be in contact with her, and fewer still if she was truly confined to her room. It has certainly happened before, at least once a month, if you know what I mean. Her personal maid occupied herself mostly in Miss Darcy's quarters, so I trust all will be well now. Even if there is talk, the truth will remain protected."

They continued to speak — her aunt definitely had a lot to share and had not lost an iota of her almost youthful enthusiasm for being at Pemberley, thought Elizabeth, fondly — until a maid came to invite them to dinner. Elizabeth assumed the others would eat in their own respective rooms, but she found herself pleased that Darcy and her uncle were already in the dining room.

Georgiana, however, chose to remain in her apartment,

with Mrs Annesley.

"I hope Georgiana is not unwell?" Elizabeth asked.

"Not at all. She just desired some solitude and rest tonight, Mrs Annesley told me," Darcy replied.

"I can easily understand that. I look forward to resting properly myself," Mr Gardiner declared. "If I can go fishing one more time before we leave, I would not want for anything else. Except for another drink," he spoke humorously.

"You may catch as many fish as you like and help yourself to as much brandy as you like, Mr Gardiner. And I shall gladly join you for both," Darcy answered in the same tone.

Elizabeth watched Darcy with heightened interest. He looked a bit pale and tired — no wonder after the week he had had, as he certainly had not slept much. But he appeared completely at ease with her uncle and aunt, and she remembered Colonel Fitzwilliam saying that Darcy was a pleasant companion amongst his family and friends. He was not only a pleasant companion, but he looked more handsome than usual, she thought, her cheeks colouring.

Dinner did not last long, as the exhaustion for some and the brandy for others curtailed the inclination for an extended conversation. They retired for the night shortly after the last course, but, while the Gardiners enjoyed their rest immediately, Elizabeth and Darcy each needed more time before the tumult of their thoughts and feelings allowed them to fall asleep, knowing that the moment of separation was fast approaching.

∞∞∞

The next day, rested and with some of their emotions settled, plans had been laid: the guests were to remain for five more days at Pemberley, enjoying the company and the beautiful summer days before returning to their homes and usual lives. Letters arrived from Netherfield, from Mr Bingley, and from Longbourn, from Mr Bennet and Jane with news from Hertfordshire, suggesting that Mr Bingley had already resumed his acquaintance with the Bennet family.

Darcy spent the remaining time mostly on estate matters and with Mr Gardiner, while Elizabeth was strengthening her acquaintance with Georgiana, having also the company of her aunt and Mrs Annesley. However, several times a day, they reunited and shared activities that pleased all of them.

Georgiana was still in low spirits, and the realisation that at least the Gardiners, Mrs Annesley, Mrs Reynolds, and very probably her maid, besides her brother and Elizabeth, were aware of her foolish escapade, made her contrite and even more subdued than usual.

Still, music remained her favourite pastime, and she agreed to practise with Elizabeth — which provoked from Elizabeth a comical rendition of Lady Catherine's strictures and advice that made Georgiana laugh for the first time since she had met her — and even play with her a few times, although not in front of the others. Conscious of not leaving Georgiana too much alone to dwell on her mistakes, Elizabeth managed to draw her out and even persuaded the girl to keep her company on her walks around the park and the gardens.

Mr and Mrs Gardiner paid some visits to their relatives in Lambton, mostly making up for the week they had not been able to do so, and on such occasions, Elizabeth was left with Darcy and Georgiana. More than once, the girl declared her regret for Elizabeth's having to leave and her hope that they would meet again soon. Elizabeth was grateful for the girl's affection and returned it most genuinely. However, she did not dare speak much of their reunion or of her possible return to Pemberley, as she did not wish to overstep her boundaries and force her presence upon Darcy if he did not express the same desire. Heaven forbid that he thought she was befriending Georgiana in order to be in his presence like other women certainly had! Her heart filled with a fresh surge of affection for Georgiana and a feeling much too strong, too overwhelming, towards Darcy to be anything but love; she barely had the courage to recognise it and admit it to herself and was still reluctant to reveal it to others. Including him.

With sorrow and heavy hearts, the last day of Elizabeth's stay at Pemberley arrived.

Mr and Mrs Gardiner went to make their farewells to their relatives and friends in Lambton, while Elizabeth remained at home with Georgiana and Darcy.

"Miss Bennet, is there anything in particular that you would like to do before your uncle and aunt return?" Darcy enquired.

She watched him, thinking that she might not see him again for a long while, and her heart became even heavier.

"Nothing in particular..." she whispered, then corrected herself. "Yes, there is something. I would like to take a last tour around the grounds. Just a last walk and a last view of the house..."

"I trust it will not be either the last tour or the last walk at Pemberley," Darcy answered. "But yes, a walk would be perfect, especially in this pleasant weather. And if we do not impose, if you do not wish for solitary contemplation, we would be happy to accompany you, would we not, Georgiana?"

"Of course not! I mean — not the last tour! You have to

promise you will come back! But yes, a walk would be lovely," the girl replied, somehow uneasy. "Only...to be honest, I have a slight headache and my back also hurts a little...no, do not worry, it is nothing but a little indisposition...not uncommon," she blushed, beseeching Elizabeth with her eyes to understand. "It will pass by dinner, I am sure. Elizabeth, would you mind? Fitzwilliam will keep you company..."

Although perfectly acceptable as an excuse, it seemed more a little scheme attempted by Georgiana to give them some moments together, but if it was so, neither was opposed to it.

"Of course I do not mind, but are you sure it is just an indisposition?"

"Yes, absolutely sure. I shall be perfectly well by the time you return."

"Very well then," Darcy concluded. "Miss Bennet, you will have to be content with my company only. I hope it will not be too tiresome."

"You should not be worried in that respect, Mr Darcy. Tiresome is the last word I would use to describe your company," Elizabeth answered with a trace of playfulness in her voice, while her heart pounded with nervous anticipation.

Although she was by now well accustomed to the grounds and knew all the paths, Elizabeth was thrilled to allow Darcy to lead her. They parted with Georgiana after reassuring themselves again that the girl would be well, and crossed the courtyard, walking side by side, their hands almost touching in the motion. Almost.

Facing the body of water, they turned left and reached the long flight of steps that climbed from the front of the manor up along the gardens, to the greenhouse, and further on. With each step, each moment, their hearts — unbeknownst to the other — raced equally wildly but in perfect harmony. The quiet beauty, the soft breeze, the music it played within the trees, the sun shimmering over the water, the slowly dawning awareness of their complete privacy, the tingling on their skin at their almost touching hands made their closeness become more and more thrilling and overwhelming.

Maybe if they felt less, they would have talked more. As it was, while their emotions grew stronger, their words grew scarce, until the silence needed to be broken and sentiments finally expressed.

"This is so beautiful. I know I keep repeating it, but it simply takes my breath away," Elizabeth said, glancing around. From the long flight of steps, leaving the orangery on their left, they turned right onto the grass, through a small grove, towards the bridge and further along the small natural course of water, to a slightly higher point which offered a stunning view over the lake and the house.

"My uncle tells me you will conduct some business affairs together in the future," Elizabeth continued.

"Yes. Besides my esteem for him, I have come to know Mr Gardiner well enough. He is a wise tradesman, with keen knowledge of the law too. Such a partner is difficult to find, therefore more valuable."

"He feels fortunate and honoured to work with you, too. That means you will meet in London as well," she added wistfully.

"Yes...I shall have to go to London anyway, there are still many details to be settled in regard to Wickham. I also need to speak to my cousin, to visit my uncle and aunt, as well as Lady Catherine. And I absolutely must visit Bingley too — he has insisted so much that I cannot refuse him."

"I am surprised his sisters joined him at Netherfield, after all," Elizabeth said.

"So am I, but I suspect both Bingley and Hurst have become more determined and less compliant lately, which I call a long-overdue improvement."

"I could not agree more. Does this mean...shall we have the opportunity to see you in Hertfordshire too?"

"Certainly. I hope to have the chance to become better acquainted with your father. Sadly, I missed the chance while living there last autumn."

"I am sure my father would like that very much too. My uncle wrote to him about your library and about the fishing parties, so I suspect you are already one of his very few favourite people," Elizabeth quipped feebly. She was in too low spirits knowing she would leave the next day. The joy of seeing her home and her family was heavily clouded by the sadness of leaving Pemberley.

"I cannot believe you leave tomorrow," he said, like he was able to read her mind.

"Indeed. I cannot believe almost three weeks have passed so quickly."

"Has it been only three weeks? It feels like you have been here for months, Miss Bennet. Or for a lifetime."

"True... When we came to Derbyshire, I did not imagine we would spend more than a few hours visiting Pemberley. To be honest, I tried to avoid it entirely, as I felt I would not be welcome here, and deservedly so."

"Three weeks ago, I could not imagine that you would want to be at Pemberley at all," he admitted his own misgivings. "Three weeks as long and eventful as a lifetime..."

A few more steps were taken in silence, and then he suddenly stopped, facing her. She stopped too, only inches from him.

"Miss Bennet, I can no longer be silent," he said precipitately. "First of all, please allow me to tell you again how grateful I am for everything you have done for my sister. I dread to imagine how things would have unfolded without you. And I fear to imagine how it will be after you leave."

"Mr Darcy, I assure you — again — there is no need for gratitude. You give me too much credit, sir. I am sure you would have settled everything properly even by yourself. You always do."

"I always do, but I have been wrong too often lately, in matters which have drastically affected the lives of people I care for. To know that not once, but twice I have failed in my duties to Georgiana and left her in the power of that scoundrel. It was you who helped me plan her rescue, who persuaded her to come back home, dealt with that despicable piece of — I can only imagine how distasteful it was for you! — and afterwards consoled her and have been a friend to her... More than a friend — the sister she always wanted. All this after I so rudely offended your sisters, and I almost ruined the happiness of your most beloved one. You repaid my arrogance and disdain with so much kindness and generosity..."

He looked so anxious to speak, so burdened with guilt and remorse, that he missed Elizabeth's embarrassment and deep blushing. She tried to interrupt, but he continued.

"I have to thank you on behalf of myself, my sister, and every member of my family whose name could have been tainted by the scandal. If they knew, if they were aware, they would thank you too. As it is, I can only convey the feelings of my sister and I...to you and your uncle and aunt, of course, to whom I shall also be forever grateful. When I think how disdainfully I spoke of them less than a year ago... You forgave my unforgivable rudeness and have done so much while I deserved so little."

She finally felt composed enough to interrupt him.

"Mr Darcy, your family has nothing to thank us for. My uncle and aunt simply acted as their character induced them to. They are good, honourable people, and if you misjudged them before you met them, since they arrived at Pemberley, it has been you who showed them kindness and generosity first. You have long remedied your past wrongs, sir, in regard to them and to my sisters."

"I hope that is true…"

"It is. It was you who forgave *my* unforgivable behaviour by welcoming me and my relatives to Pemberley. As for myself, I only thought of Georgiana…and of you. Seeing you that morning in the library, so completely devastated, made me wish to take your grief away. Nobody's sadness has ever touched my heart so deeply."

"Nobody's company and support has given me so much comfort and strength," he said. "I know I am being selfish, but I cannot help but wonder how I shall bear your absence. I have become so accustomed to greeting you every morning, having you close every day, having the privilege of seeing your smiles, hearing your laughter, seeing you with Georgiana, or simply knowing that you are within the same house as I, that I already dread the moment when I shall miss it."

"I shall miss Pemberley too. And you and Georgiana, of course," she admitted, trying not to allow the emotion in her soul to alter her voice. "Georgiana already asked me when we would meet again. If only Hertfordshire was closer to Derbyshire, I could visit more often," she concluded as a little joke. "Sadly, we cannot move either county."

"We cannot, indeed," Darcy replied with earnestness and gravity. But…"

He paused for a moment, then took a deep breath as

though he was inhaling the courage to continue. When he did, his voice was slightly trembling with emotions he could not control.

"Miss Bennet, for many days now I have been torn between speaking my mind and protecting your comfort. I do not wish to force you to listen to my words while you are my guest, or to accept my confession out of pity or obligation. As such, I shall rely — again — on your strength and honesty. I know you are too generous to trifle with me. I know your feelings have changed since last April, but to what extent, I cannot be sure. My feelings and wishes are unchanged — no, that is not true — they are deeper and stronger. But what you desire is more important to me. If you only wish to remain friends, one word from you will silence me forever on this subject."

He was relieved to finally unburden his soul, but frightened that his confession might bring back the pain he had just healed from.

She listened to him, hopeful, and he could not be sure whether her crimson face was due to embarrassment or pleasure.

"Regardless, you will always be welcomed at Pemberley, and you will always have my and my sister's gratitude and esteem," he ended, struggling to see the answer in her eyes before it was voiced.

"Mr Darcy, I...my feelings have changed so much since last April that for a while even I was not certain of their extent and nature. But now I have no more doubts, and my wishes are clear..."

It was her turn to pause and his to wait fearfully.

"I do not want to be welcomed when I visit Pemberley. I do not want your friendship, your gratitude, or even your esteem, Mr Darcy. I want your ardent admiration and love, and I want you to be certain of mine. I want to learn more about those feelings that could not be repressed. I want to not have to leave Pemberley, or you — so I could never miss you."

She had no time — and no desire — to reflect on the propriety of her words. She spoke them as they came from her heart and her mind, and rejoiced in the expression of heartfelt delight spread over his handsome face.

He took her hands in his, as he had done before, and placed them on his chest.

"You have them all, Miss Bennet...my beloved Elizabeth. You have my most ardent love and admiration, except my feelings are now completely unrepressed. If it depended on me, I would never allow you to leave Pemberley and my arms. But my happiness is still not free from worries, so I must ask, only to hear the answer from your lips: Would you do me the honour of becoming my wife?"

"I would...I will. Surely you cannot doubt it, Mr Darcy. Not any longer, Fitzwilliam."

"Not any longer, my dearest, loveliest Elizabeth," he admitted, closing his arms around her.

Although the trees offered them some privacy, they could still be seen from Pemberley's windows, which did cause the master some restraint in expressing himself as his ardent love tempted him. However, despite being a gentleman of honour and strong self-control, Mr Darcy claimed — and was happily granted — the first timid, tender, gentle kiss, followed by a few others, less timid, more daring but as tender, until he felt capable of separating from his betrothed.

Sometime later, arm in arm, still intoxicated by the sweet taste of shared love and overwhelmed by their understanding, they walked back towards Pemberley, making plans about how to proceed in revealing their engagement to their families and friends, especially to Mr Bennet, whose blessing they hoped for and sought.

Chapter 14

The betrothed couple was so overjoyed that they could not stop smiling all the way back to the house. Being in full view, the gentleman having kindly offered his arm and the lady having cheerfully accepted it, they kept an almost proper distance from each other, but the brief caresses they shared, the scent and taste of each other, the awareness of the feelings aroused inside them, the relief of finally being certain their love was mutual, the expectations of the future now easily foreseen — all caused such a delight as neither of them had felt before.

The knowledge that Elizabeth would leave the following day lost its melancholy, replaced by the contentment of the certainty that she would return soon, as the mistress of Pemberley and of the master's heart.

With the little composure they still possessed, they discussed the best way to give the news to their closest relatives — Georgiana and the Gardiners. Considering Mr Gardiner was Elizabeth's guardian during her journey, Darcy suggested speaking to him first and asking for his consent, then sharing it with the ladies, and Elizabeth readily acquiesced.

According to the plan, Darcy invited Mr Gardiner to join him in the library as soon as they entered the house. Darcy felt slightly nervous in the solemnity of the moment and thought he might need a drink before he started, so he proposed one to Mr Gardiner, who accepted and enjoyed his brandy with apparent serenity.

"Mr Gardiner, there is something of great importance for which I need your support. And your approval…"

"Mr Darcy, you already have my support and approval for anything you might need."

"Thank you…but this is different…I…in short, I asked Miss Bennet for her hand in marriage, and she generously granted it to me. I am applying to you since her father is not present. I plan to address Mr Bennet too, as soon as possible."

Mr Gardiner showed less surprise than Darcy expected, but he stood up and bowed formally as he replied, "Mr Darcy, I would never refuse you anything that you did me the favour of asking for. I confess I have noticed your partiality for my niece for some time. In fact, from almost the beginning of our acquaintance. I also suspect your affection was formed prior to our arrival at Pemberley and has lasted for some duration."

"You are very observant, sir! I should not have doubted it, of course. However, only recently have I been so fortunate as to win Miss Bennet's heart. Due to my past behaviour, her opinion of me was not particularly good."

"Yes, yes, I remember some of your past misunderstandings. In marrying my niece Elizabeth, I am certain you are making a wise choice, which will bring a happy and fulfilled life to both of you. You are the best of gentlemen, and I am aware of how fortunate my niece is, considering the differences between your situations in life. Choosing Lizzy as your wife shows wisdom and deep knowledge of human nature, as well as an excellent taste in ladies if I may say so," Mr Gardiner concluded with a little humour.

"I feel fortunate for being accepted, sir. Before I met Miss Bennet, I was rather oblivious to my faults, and she helped me see the truth of my own insufficiency. It was not an easy journey, I assure you."

"I imagine as much," Mr Gardiner replied.

"I admit I am a little worried about how Mr and Mrs Bennet will receive the news and respond to my application. My behaviour towards them has been marked by despicable arrogance, I have long realised that. Sadly, I have no time to make amends, and I fear their rejection. Were I the father, I would not allow my daughter to marry a man with such rude manners and behaviour."

Mr Gardiner smiled and sipped from his glass. "My brother Bennet will be utterly shocked and wary, and he will question this marriage which seems hasty. Luckily, Lizzy will have the chance to speak to her father before you. I shall also write to him, so by the time you address him, he will be rather accustomed to the notion. But I suspect he will give you a hard time, and you will have to bear his sarcasm and wit for a long while. Bear in mind that Lizzy is his favourite. However, I suspect he will be interested enough to come and see your much-praised library, so he will overcome any objections."

Darcy widened his eyes in alarm, and Mr Gardiner laughed.

"I just gave you a taste of what you will have to suffer from my brother. His great enjoyment is to make sport of those around him, even those he loves. So be forewarned."

"I see...I believe I shall be prepared," Darcy replied, thinking he might need his drink after all. "Miss Bennet herself has censured me and taken me to task more severely than anyone ever has, so I doubt it can be any worse."

"As for my sister Bennet, you have nothing to worry about. Being tall, handsome, and so rich, you will easily get her approval," Mr Gardiner ended, very amused, and Darcy wondered whether he was being serious or was still jesting.

Soon after that conversation, they joined the ladies, and another announcement followed for Mrs Gardiner and Georgiana. Elizabeth was still not comfortable enough to speak about her new felicity, so it was Darcy again who gave the news. However, his sister and Elizabeth's aunt seemed more glad than surprised, offering their congratulations warmly, leaving no doubts about their approval.

"My dear Elizabeth, I could not be happier!" Georgiana said, embracing her tearfully. "I prayed and hoped that my brother would ask you before you left. I was afraid I would lose you, but now I know you will marry soon and return to be my sister."

Such an outburst from a restrained, shy girl was heart melting, and Elizabeth held her tight, feeling her own eyes moisten.

"My dear Georgiana, you would not have lost me anyway. By marrying your brother, I could not love you more, as I have already loved you as a sister for a long time now. But you must be warned — you will be granted four more sisters, who will surely come to love you too, but only my dear Jane will not be a challenge to your serenity."

At Georgiana's worried expression, Elizabeth laughed and stroked her hair. "And another fair warning — being related to the Bennet family, you will have to become accustomed to teasing."

"It seems we both have to become accustomed to teasing, my dear," Darcy interjected. "I presume I shall be the preferred recipient of such, much more than you. And I fully deserve it."

∞ ∞ ∞

Three and half weeks after they arrived in Derbyshire, the Gardiners and Elizabeth left the place that had changed their lives as if in a dream they would never have dared to believe might become reality — until it did.

The farewell from Darcy was emotional, but not sad, as he was expected to arrive in Hertfordshire in less than a fortnight, and Georgiana would follow later on. The Darcys planned to travel shortly after their guests' departure, to London first, as he needed to visit his solicitor and changes needed to be made at the townhouse before he returned in the company of his wife.

Of the servants, only Mrs Annesley and Mrs Reynolds were informed about the engagement, in confidence. Although both expected such news — as Mr Darcy, they both knew, would never display such particular attention to a lady unless he had a serious inclination towards her — Mrs Reynolds could not help embracing her master with the affection of a mother. Secretly, she had feared that the most excellent of men — the best master and the best landlord — might do what was expected of him and marry someone of higher consequence but with insufficient affection and warmth of the heart to make him happy. Seeing him in the company of pretty and cheerfully witty Miss Bennet, and knowing he had chosen her to stand by his side, was a reason for relief and joy and hope — and the happiness on his and her countenance left no room for doubt that a great deal of affection was shared.

Elizabeth's departure brought such emptiness and longing to both that Darcy speeded up their travelling plans. While Georgiana would remain in London with Mrs Annesley, Darcy was determined to reach Netherfield — and Longbourn — at the earliest possible time. Once he had Mr Bennet's blessing, he and Elizabeth might decide either to apply for a common licence or marry at Longbourn after waiting for the banns to be read.

In addition, other urgent and important matters that needed his attention had to be accomplished, together with those in regard to Wickham's transfer to the new regiment. Darcy felt somehow relieved to have purchased all Wickham's debts and have him at his mercy. The threat of being thrown into debtors' prison was frightening even for a man with as little honour as Wickham and would likely temper any further attempts to trouble Darcy. But impatience and opportunity could push Wickham to act, braving the possibility of finding himself at the Fleet or Marshalsea, despite the reputation of the horrors inside, and Darcy felt it would be better if the scoundrel was enrolled under strict orders.

He had to present the news of his engagement to his family and — except for Colonel Fitzwilliam — he expected some opposition or at least some questioning from the earl and even stronger objections from Lady Catherine, whose reaction to the collapse of her own plans and wishes might be dangerous for his equanimity. He could have written to them, but he felt he owed it to them, as his closest family on his mother's side, to disclose his decision in person.

He should arrange for the announcement in the papers. He knew his few but genuine friends would understand his choice and approve of it. Also, many of his acquaintances in the ton would loathe his marriage — mostly those whose hopes of an alliance with him would thus be dashed — and most likely reject Elizabeth. There would surely be a civil reception, and she would be treated properly as fitted her position as Mrs Darcy, albeit with cold politeness, and he would always be there to protect her. Not that he doubted her abilities. But it would take time and patience and maybe some well-chosen allies before she was recognised as the worthy, exceptional, and accomplished woman she was and be treated with the genuine respect and admiration she deserved.

However, nothing could ruin Darcy's present felicity, and the prospect of having Elizabeth with him, by his side, in the privacy of their home, their apartments, every day for the rest of his life, was the strongest inducement to defy any obstacles.

The journey back home was not easy for Elizabeth either. As the carriage took her away from Darcy and Pemberley, she had the time to reflect on everything that had occurred — from the day she had arrived at Pemberley, fearing unreasonably that Darcy might throw her out of his home, to the moment she had enjoyed the first proof of his ardent love.

Being Darcy's wife would be pure bliss, she knew that. They would surely not always agree on everything, and they would certainly argue often, but she knew their nature and character would complete and complement each other. And she knew he was the only man in the world perfectly suited to her — as she had already told him the night before she left, in a short, private, and not entirely proper interlude in the library.

However, being Mrs Darcy and the mistress of Pemberley meant countless responsibilities attached to that position, as well as hard work and much to learn so that she could accomplish everything that was expected of her.

As for her reception in society, Elizabeth knew it would not be easy. All the women who had aspired to gain Darcy's attention, as well as their families, would despise her and treat her with arrogance and cold politeness — at best. Also, Lady Catherine's reaction when faced with the end of her own designs of uniting her daughter to her nephew would certainly be spectacular and fearsome.

But the recollections of Darcy's warm embrace and the safety she felt in his arms, of his tender yet passionate kisses and caresses, of his intense stares whose meaning she understood now without a doubt, gave her strength to bear any opposition. She was ready, eager, and thrilled to become Mrs Darcy — his wife.

∞∞∞∞

Elizabeth was keeping her eyes closed, the thrill of the last few days at Pemberley giving way to a satisfied exhaustion.

Suddenly, she felt all her senses awaken when she felt *his* presence, his nearness, his warmth, his scent surrounding her. Dizzy and overwhelmed, she tried to pry her eyes open, only to meet his burning stare, dark pools of liquid passion and promises that did not need words. She felt his hands cupping her face, his thumbs barely there, a gossamer touch along her cheeks, jaw, and chin, then finally tracing her lips, which parted in sweet torturous anticipation. She was floating, insensible to everything but the feeling of his fingers on her skin and the expectation of his lips.

But the awaited touch did not come. His fingers still brushing her lips, she felt more than she heard his ardent whispers, his lips and hot breath tantalising the delicate skin behind her ear, tasting the sweetness of her neck while one of his hands moved slowly to her back, pressing her gently towards him. She leant eagerly against him, rejoicing in the pleasure of his closeness and tender strength, whispering her own passionate pleas, until finally his lips claimed hers, crushing her moan in a long awaited kiss that made her burn all over and made every fibre of her body and soul vibrate with love and exhilaration.

"Lizzy? Lizzy my dear, are you well?" She heard a voice that startled her, and she glanced around, confused, still dizzy, her cheeks burning. She realised she was in the carriage that was taking her away from *him*, and had to bear her uncle and aunt's enquiring looks.

"Did you have a bad dream? You look a bit flushed," Mrs Gardiner insisted, and Elizabeth's face burnt even more.

"No, no, I just... I am sorry I fell asleep, but it seems I was more tired than I thought," she replied, trying to sound composed.

"I imagined as much, my dear," Mr Gardiner interjected. "I was telling your aunt that I look forward to hearing what brother Bennet will have to say about your engagement," he added as the carriage brought them closer and closer to Longbourn.

"I look forward to seeing the children — I hope they have not given poor Jane too much trouble," Mrs Gardiner replied.

"Uncle, will you talk to Papa first? Or would you like me to do it?"

"I shall — of course, Lizzy. I would not lose such an opportunity for entertainment. I wonder if he will believe me, though."

Mr Gardiner was in an exceedingly good disposition, despite the long and tedious journey of which Mrs Gardiner and Elizabeth were already tired. They were all happy when the carriage stopped and the Gardiner children, as well as all the Bennet girls, burst out to greet them.

A few minutes of bustle followed, with cries of joy, questions, laughter, demands of gifts, and embraces, until everyone finally entered the house. The only one who stayed calm and silent, with a reproachful and disinterested stare at the clamour, was Mr Bennet, who greeted Elizabeth and the Gardiners, then stepped aside from the din.

"My dear brother and sister, how happy I am to see you! And you too, Lizzy! You will never guess what extraordinary news I have! Mr Bingley returned to Netherfield two weeks ago! Without any notice, nothing, we just found out one day that he had opened the house, and then, in a blink of an eye, he was here!"

"Yes, we knew that, Sister," Mr Gardiner answered, while Elizabeth held Jane's arm affectionately. "We were at Pemberley with Mr Bingley, remember? We spoke to him there, and he informed us of his plan to return. He even asked Lizzy whether the neighbours would approve of it."

"Did he?" Mrs Bennet cried. "And what did you tell him, Lizzy? Oh, never mind, it does not really matter since he is here! But wait! There is more! Earlier today, he proposed to Jane! They are engaged to be married! Dear Lord, bless me! I still cannot believe it. I completely lost hope when he left last winter. And now — here he is! How fortunate for Jane and for all of us! Is it not the happiest and most incredible news ever? Have you ever heard anything more astonishing?"

"I would not call it the most incredible or the most astonishing," Mr Gardiner answered with a mischievous grin, while his wife and Elizabeth were already embracing and congratulating Jane. "But it is very happy news. I wish you all the best, Jane, you deserve it. He is an excellent man, and you are as beautiful as you are sweet and kind! Perfect for each other."

"And five thousand a year!" Mrs Bennet continued. "Tomorrow morning, I am going to Meryton to tell my sister Phillips and call on Mrs Long and Lady Lucas! She is so annoying as she keeps talking about Charlotte and that tedious Mr Collins! Like anyone would care! And only a month ago she claimed Mr

Bingley would never return to Netherfield! Wait until I tell her!"

"Oh, and Lizzy, you will be shocked to hear something else even more unbelievable!" Lydia cried. "Your favourite Mr Wickham has left the regiment and disappeared! Denny and Chamberlayne and Pratt said he had many debts, but I'm sure they are only jealous because Mr Wickham was more handsome than them! We were all dumbfounded when we found out! Are you not, Lizzy?"

"I am sorry to interrupt such universal amazement," Mr Bennet finally interjected, "but you may continue it at dinner. I need a rest, so I am going to the library now. Would you join me, Brother?"

"Gladly. In fact, I was about to suggest it myself. Amazement is surely easier to bear over a glass of brandy," Mr Gardiner replied with a grin and a meaningful glance at his wife and Elizabeth.

∞ ∞ ∞

The hubbub continued in the drawing room, with Mrs Bennet asking questions about the journey and allowing no time for answers, Lydia and Kitty complaining about Wickham's disappearance, Mary unsuccessfully trying to intervene in the conversation, and the children relating countless details of their stay at Longbourn to their mother.

Eventually, Mr Gardiner returned and signalled to Elizabeth that she was wanted. She smiled but was not without some anxiety as she entered the library, looking at her father. He was sitting in his chair, in a befuddled state of mind, frowning with preoccupation.

"Papa?"

"Yes, Lizzy. Come, sit down, child. I must admit that, after the conversation with your uncle, I have discovered new meanings of the words astonishment and amazement. And unbelievable. And stupefaction. And stupor..."

Elizabeth leant towards him and kissed his cheeks.

"Papa, do not be so solemn and severe, it is really not the case, I promise you. It does sound unbelievable, but if you knew more details..."

"Well then, do humour me, child. There is nothing I want more than details to spare me from feeling like an oblivious simpleton. When you left Longbourn less than a month ago, you had Wickham as a friend and Darcy as your worst enemy. How can I not feel that you have deceived me? You have returned engaged to Darcy, and I learn that Wickham is the worst sort of a despicable scoundrel — which, to be sure, is the least surprising part for me of everything I have been told."

Mr Bennet's voice became agitated, while Elizabeth's smile remained still, trying to calm him.

"Papa, you are no simpleton, and I have certainly not deceived you. I was a complete fool for trusting Wickham's claims, and yes, I do remember you teasing me about him. But during my stay in Kent, although having several harsh arguments with Mr Darcy and accusing him of many flaws, my opinion about him and about Wickham changed."

"I see...now I only have to understand how it happened that, after the arguments and accusations you bestowed upon Darcy, he chose to propose marriage to you. Perhaps he wishes to have his revenge against you, although this would be a rather drastic measure."

Elizabeth laughed again. "I doubt he seeks revenge, Papa.

However, returning engaged to Mr Darcy was the last thing I could imagine when I left Longbourn. I expected him to throw me from his estate if he found me there. Instead, he was nothing but polite and friendly to us. His behaviour, his manners have—"

"Yes, I heard," interrupted Mr Bennet impatiently. "Brother Gardiner praised Darcy so much that I wondered whether he would not have welcomed a marriage proposal from him too."

"Papa! You are truly incorrigible. As soon as you come to know Mr Darcy well enough, you will have to admit that none of the praise was undeserved. He is truly the best of men. I am so fortunate that he is generous and kind and found the strength to love me against my prejudiced and awful behaviour towards him."

"But how could he come to love you in less than a month? How could he decide to marry you after such a short while? What if whatever induced him to propose is gone just as fast and you are both miserable for the rest of your lives? Can I allow this, Lizzy?"

"Dear Papa, you have no reason to worry. He did not begin to love me a month ago, nor did he propose to me on the impulse of a moment. His feelings and steadfastness have been under the most difficult probation. I shall tell you all, but you must promise to keep the secret unless he chooses to reveal it to you. I have not told another soul, except for Jane."

"Now you are scaring me, and I fear I shall be further amazed, Lizzy. Let me pour another drink — I am sure I will need it."

Elizabeth's narration about the rejected marriage proposal stunned Mr Bennet even more than he had believed it would. The notion that his favourite daughter had the audacity to refuse such a man and that she accused him so undeservingly were reasons for both pride and upset for him.

Darcy's transformation, his improved manners, and his friendly behaviour towards Elizabeth and the Gardiners impressed him and aroused his amazement the most. When Elizabeth finished her narrative, he needed some time to process the story. At length, he spoke.

"My dear Lizzy, I would not have been so generous, you know. I would not have forgiven a woman who rejected me so uncivilly, and provided that I eventually did, I would never have proposed to her again. In fact, I am sure that few men — if any — would."

"I know, Papa. That is why I called myself grateful and fortunate."

"But…you do realise that half of the ton will hate you. Including Mr Bingley's sisters, I assume."

"And Lady Catherine, to be sure," Elizabeth laughed again. "I am well aware, but being Mr Darcy's wife will provide me with enough reasons for happiness and gratification to oppose and disregard any disapproval. After all, his approval and regard matter the most."

Mr Bennet shook his head and sipped more from his drink.

"Very well, Lizzy — be it as you wish. I confess I am still astounded, and I shall probably need a long time to comprehend all I have heard and to accept everything that has occurred. For now, I shall have several more drinks with your uncle to help me get some sleep."

"I am sure you and Mr Darcy will get along well, Papa. Just receive him with an open heart and mind. He knows his past errors, just as I know mine."

"I shall do just that, Lizzy. Now let us go to dinner. By the by, do you intend to share your news with your mother and sisters tonight?"

"Oh no! Certainly not, Papa. There is nothing to be said until Mr Darcy himself comes to speak to you and you give your blessing. Besides, I would not want to ruin the pleasure of Jane and Mr Bingley's engagement. They must be the centre of attention for now."

"Excellent thinking. I could not bear more excitement tonight, and I plan to be away from home when you give the news of your engagement to your mother. If she cried so much when Bingley proposed, in Darcy's case, the uproar would surely be heard in Meryton and beyond!"

"Dear Papa, you truly are irredeemable. I have missed you so much."

"I missed you too, my Lizzy," he said, briefly kissing her hand. "I do not even want to consider that soon you will leave Longbourn forever."

"Let us not be sad about that, Papa. It will not be forever. We shall visit often, and you will visit us. I cannot wait for you to see Pemberley!"

"Yes, yes, your uncle told me about it. I only have one question still: What induced you to fall in love with Darcy in the end? It happened at Pemberley, obviously. Was it the park, the library, or the image of his ten thousand pounds?"

"Papa, you may tease me as much as you want, and you might not even like the answer. I did recognise my love for him at Pemberley, but it was certainly him being tall and handsome and kind and affectionate, and confessing his ardent love to me, and holding my hands, and, when nobody was watching, even ki..."

Mr Bennet looked at his favourite daughter alarmed, in disbelief.

"Have you lost your mind, child? Why are you telling your father such things?"

Elizabeth kissed his cheek with another laugh.

"Well, Papa, you must learn to accept others making sport at your expense, too. I am almost as good at teasing as you are. I hope your nerves are strong enough to bear it."

Elizabeth's cheerfulness was contagious, and she held her father's arm tightly, while he only shook his head, already knowing he would miss her terribly.

Chapter 15

The Gardiners remained at Longbourn only two more days, then returned to London. When they departed, Elizabeth lost most of the people with whom she could discuss Darcy; only her father remained, but he mostly teased her while he became more and more accustomed to the idea of her marriage. After sound reflection, she decided not to tell Jane about her engagement. Her sister was overjoyed, blooming from her own felicity, and it was only fair that she could rejoice in her happiness only. Mr Bingley was a daily visitor to Longbourn, and he indeed spoke about Darcy quite often.

Elizabeth only saw Mrs Hurst and Miss Bingley once, when they had tea together after the announcement of their brother's engagement, which they treated with visible disapproval and disdain. The meeting was as cold and awkward as expected, with discussion of Pemberley and Georgiana, whose health was 'a major preoccupation' for the Bingley sisters. They mentioned that they had received 'a long and detailed letter from dear Georgiana, whose friendship was invaluable to them'.

Elizabeth chose to make few comments, attempting to hide her smiles and amusement at their imaginary grossly exaggerated intimacy with Georgiana, allowing Mr Bingley to struggle with concealing the truth and temper his sisters. To her, it was more entertaining to imagine the sisters' reaction when they would find out about her own engagement to Darcy. *That* was a scene she looked forward to witnessing.

Unlike their previous stay at Netherfield, Mr Hurst was a pleasant companion, showing respectful courtesy towards the Bennet ladies and some censure towards his wife and sister-in-law's rudeness. He was, though, not willing to produce any disagreement or argument, so he remained loyal to his nonchalant attitude.

With the regiment moved to Brighton, Meryton was rather peaceful. Lydia received a note from her friend, Colonel Forster's wife, describing all the entertainment she enjoyed and regretting Lydia was not there. Lydia cried and whined several times a day, together with Kitty, but Mrs Bennet, caught in the fever of the upcoming wedding, remained indifferent to their complaints until she became irritated and dismissed them completely. In Mrs Forster's letters there was also some mention of Wickham's appalling actions towards fellow officers — and some others were revealed in regard to his behaviour even in Meryton — but Mrs Bennet dismissed those too, as she did not want to ruin her disposition with any unpleasantness.

From Kent, the news of Charlotte Collins expecting an heir arrived by way of a letter her mother came to share, but — to Lady Lucas's chagrin — it was quickly disregarded and overshadowed by the preparations for Jane Bennet's wedding to Mr Bingley.

Elizabeth received letters from Georgiana and from Mrs Gardiner. Her friend informed her about their arrival in London and mentioned that she would not come to Hertfordshire until her brother had settled all his affairs. Her aunt informed her that Mr and Miss Darcy were expected to dine with them one evening, and that Mr Gardiner had already met Mr Darcy for business purposes at his gentlemen's club.

With every passing day, the waiting became more difficult for Elizabeth. She was eager to find out how Darcy's plans progressed, but mostly, she missed him. Mr Bingley — a dinner companion for the family almost every other evening — had received letters from him, but he only expected Darcy 'as soon as possible'.

On a rainy September afternoon, just before dinner, the sound of a carriage and her racing heart announced to Elizabeth that her wait had ended. When the servant announced Darcy, Elizabeth glanced at her father, noticing his slight disquiet.

Mr Bingley, as a true part of the family, immediately hurried to welcome his friend, introducing him with unrestrained pleasure.

The Bennet ladies — even Jane, Elizabeth noticed with a clenching heart — received Darcy with either suspicion for the older ones, or indifference for the younger, but generally little expectation of pleasure. Even though Mr Bingley and the Gardiners had spoken highly of Darcy, the recollection of the proud and arrogant gentleman they had met a year ago and his intolerable slight against Lizzy, made Mrs Bennet and her daughters prudent and reluctant.

However, Darcy entered, and the first change, visible immediately, was his friendly greeting and his countenance — warmer and brighter than ever before.

The guest glanced at Elizabeth several times, but, as propriety required, he addressed himself to her parents.

"Mr Bennet, Mrs Bennet! It is a pleasure to see you again. Please forgive me for appearing unannounced at this hour. I shall not bother you long. I have just arrived from London and wanted to greet you all and to present Mr Bennet with a letter from Mr Gardiner, then I shall go to Netherfield."

"You are not bothering us, Mr Darcy," Mr Bennet said. "You are welcome, and since your friend is here, I hope you are not too eager to be at Netherfield. We would be happy for you to stay for dinner if you do not have other plans."

"I do not, but I do not want to disturb *your* plans," he said, with another stolen look at Elizabeth.

"Nonsense! You are not disturbing us at all! And there is enough food for one more, I am sure. Mrs Bennet's dinners are always fabulous!" Mr Bingley said enthusiastically.

"Oh, I am just trying my best, considering our limited possibilities in the countryside," Mrs Bennet answered with unusual modesty. "But I am certain a man accustomed to all fineries would call my dishes tolerable, at the most."

The sharp arrow with a poisoned tip sent towards Darcy took everyone by surprise. He looked disconcerted at first, then, causing even more surprise to Elizabeth and her father, he bowed his head acknowledging the point and answered with a hint of a smile, "What I found 'tolerable' last year when I did not pay careful attention and my judgment was faulty, turned out to be wonderful on closer consideration. As for my time at Longbourn, I trust I shall share the same opinion as Bingley."

His words sounded a little too complicated to be fully understood — except for Elizabeth and her father, who smiled at his discreet confession. However, his voice, his countenance, and his obvious admittance of error were enough for Mrs Bennet to overcome her past grudge. After all, the man was her future son-in-law's best friend, and she did not wish to argue with him any longer.

"Mr Darcy, you said you had a letter for me?" Mr Bennet

intervened. "May I offer you a drink in my library while I see what my brother has to say?"

"Yes, of course! Thank you," he mumbled, following the host and glancing at Elizabeth one more time, while Mrs Bennet wondered what on earth Darcy was thanking her husband for.

The minutes passed torturously slowly for Elizabeth, and she made an effort to remain still on her chair; she listened to the conversation but understood little of it, and when the servant came to call her to the library, she almost jumped from her seat. She turned the doorknob with increasing nervousness, and inside, she found the two beloved gentlemen sitting on opposite sides of Mr Bennet's desk, each with a glass of brandy in front of them.

Darcy hurried to her and took her hand, leading her towards a chair.

"Well, my dear, I have spoken to Mr Darcy at length," Mr Bennet declared. "It was quite an entertaining conversation. I believe his main flaw is his tendency to take too much upon himself, which is a good balance for others who rarely take responsibility for anything. That would be me."

"Papa! That is not true!"

"Yes, it is, and I know it too well. It is a blessing that both you and Jane found good, reliable young gentlemen to have as husbands, otherwise, my poor skills in managing the estate would have left you at Mr Collins's mercy. Fortunately, all ended well and with little effort on my part. I do feel guilty, but I am sure it will not last long."

"Papa, now *you* are too hard on yourself. You are an excellent man and a most loving father."

"That I try to be, Lizzy, but loving my daughters is not enough. Regardless, let us return to Mr Darcy's application, which still amazes me, even after I have granted my consent."

"Mr Bennet wishes to know whether we are certain we want to marry," Darcy explained with an open smile, looking her in the eyes in his earnest manner. "I assured him I had never been more certain of anything in my life."

"I have no doubts, Papa," Elizabeth answered her father, but her eyes were locked with Darcy's. "I thought I had already convinced you by now."

"I felt it was my duty to ask one more time. If so, I am giving you both my blessing. Have you decided on a wedding date yet?"

"I shall agree to any date Miss Elizabeth decides," Darcy said. "I only hope to marry in time for us all to spend Christmas at Pemberley, if you have not made other plans. Mr and Mrs Gardiner were quite thrilled by the notion, but it depends on your decision."

"To be honest," Mr Bennet interjected, "once you announce your engagement to your mother, I would rather have you married as soon as possible, as I expect her to speak of nothing else, every day, every hour, to everyone. She will finish with Jane's wedding and go on about yours, Lizzy. What would be even better is a double wedding, so we can avoid half the clamour," he concluded mostly in jest.

Elizabeth and Darcy's gazes met again and locked for a moment.

"Actually, Papa," Elizabeth answered, "that is a lovely idea. I would love a double wedding, if nobody were opposed to it. There is a full month left, it should be enough time."

"Are you really considering it?" Mr Bennet asked, somewhat surprised.

"Yes. Are you, Mr Darcy?"

"Of course! I mean, if Miss Bennet agrees, and Bingley most certainly will, it would be perfectly agreeable to me."

"Perfectly agreeable to me, too," the host replied. "Lizzy dear, let us not give any news to your mother until after dinner, lest it would be ruined entirely."

"Very well, Papa. It can wait until tomorrow morning. Except I wish to speak to Jane later tonight."

"And I shall talk to Bingley tonight, at Netherfield," Darcy added.

"Excellent. I am glad we had such a successful conversation. Now let us join the others — dinner should be ready."

They walked together to the door, but just a moment before they left the library, Mr Bennet spoke.

"Mr Darcy, whenever you have the time and disposition, there is still something I am dying to understand. You met Lizzy last October and refused to dance with her since she was barely tolerable to you. Then you argued all the time — she told me. Then, in November you left and did not see her again until you travelled to Kent, where you argued again and then you proposed marriage to her. She refused you and accused you of a thousand sins, then you did not see her for several more months, and then you proposed to her the second time. How is it possible that Lizzy made you fall in love with her by being absent most of the time and acting impertinent the rest of it?"

Darcy stared at him in disbelief, while Elizabeth felt a pang of unease too. Her father's sharp summary of their story, while not exactly comprehensive, was disturbingly accurate and difficult to explain. Mr Bennet did not even wait for an answer, continuing to walk until Darcy's voice stopped him.

"Mr Bennet, although I suspect your enquiry was mostly

meant to tease me and make sport at my expense, I shall not let it pass without a response. I fell in love with your daughter almost from the beginning of our acquaintance because of the liveliness of her mind, her wit, her sharp intellect, her kind heart, her unassuming manners, her bravery, and a lot of other reasons. I refused to admit my feelings because at the time I considered I could only choose a wife close to my circle, with a situation similar to mine. Then, although I left, I never stopped thinking of her. When we met again, I decided she was my perfect choice for a wife. However, my arrogance forbade me from seeing that I was far from her perfect choice for a husband!"

He paused a moment, looking at Elizabeth, who was gazing at him, mesmerised. Then he caught his breath and continued.

"Her refusal offended me, enraged me, made me resentful, but also forced me to look at myself in a mirror of truth and accept that most of her words were true. So I had to choose to either return to my old selfish ways or try to remedy my errors. When I met her again at Pemberley, the final decision was easily made."

Saying that, he took Elizabeth's hand and briefly brought it to his lips. The expression of love in her bright eyes and the dazzling smile she bestowed on him made the embarrassment of his long speech completely worth the while. Mr Bennet shook his head, obviously affected by emotions as well, cleared his throat, and replied, "Well then…I think there is not much more to say. I surely do not have any more questions, all is crystal clear. Should we go to dinner now?"

"Gladly, sir," Darcy agreed, then, as Mr Bennet stepped forward, he placed another kiss on Elizabeth's hand and released it only a moment before they entered the dining room.

∞∞∞

Dinner was most pleasant, and, because of the lively conversation, mostly from Mrs Bennet and Mr Bingley, nobody noticed that Elizabeth and Mr Bennet, preoccupied with their own thoughts, were less voluble than usual. Both sat on either side of Darcy, and there was not much direct conversation.

Darcy's silence was not surprising, but his amiable manners and several compliments to Mrs Bennet had been so genuine that by the end of the evening, he had made a more favourable impression on Lydia, Kitty, and Mary.

The two gentlemen left Longbourn close to midnight. As soon as the family retired, Elizabeth shared her happy news with Jane, whose reaction was everything she had hoped for. Jane's rapture at having Darcy as her brother was expressed with many tears of joy and embraces, and the agreement to a double wedding came immediately, leaving the two sisters' happiness complete. Elizabeth only needed to prepare for the conversation with her mother the next morning, and then she would have the liberty to enjoy her engagement with her betrothed, to whom she had still so much to confess of her own feelings.

At Netherfield, Darcy spoke to Bingley over several glasses of brandy that the latter needed in order to accept the story. Bingley was surprised, even doubtful at first, although he admitted he had long noticed Darcy's partiality for Elizabeth. The notion that his friend — chased by so many young, and not so young, heiresses of the ton — had decided to marry his future sister-in-law, the daughter of an insignificant country squire, was something Bingley would not have contemplated only a month ago. But since it had happened, Bingley declared he was thrilled to share his wedding with his friend.

The only worry, which needed another brandy or three,

was the daunting task of imparting the news to his sister the next morning — something for which he demanded Darcy's assistance and support.

Chapter 16

Despite the tasty dishes and artful presentation, there was not much appetite for breakfast at Netherfield.

Caroline Bingley was particularly irritated, and she expressed it more than adequately with every huff, tap of her slippers, or every brusque gesture. Darcy tried to ignore anything that annoyed him while drinking only coffee; he had a bad headache after too many drinks with Bingley and too little sleep the night before. While not exactly in low spirits — how could he be? — he only waited for a reasonable hour so he could call at Longbourn.

He was prepared for uproar there too, as Mrs Bennet was about to receive the news that morning, and Mr Bennet had warned him that the lady's reaction — whether positive or negative — would be strong and loud.

Darcy was still smiling to himself as he recollected his encounter with Mr Bennet and the reunion with Elizabeth. After missing her for more than a fortnight, the sight of her, her smiles, her closeness, her touches, her scent were all intoxicating. And the realisation that he would marry her in a month was beyond thrilling.

"Upon my word, Mr Darcy, you look quite ill," Miss Bingley said. "It seems dinner at Longbourn did not sit too well with you, which is not surprising."

"There was nothing wrong with dinner, I assure you, Miss Bingley. I apologise if my appearance displeases you," Darcy replied.

"It is not your appearance that displeases me, sir, but your actions. Forgive me if I offended you, but as an intimate friend, it is my duty to speak my mind to your benefit. I had always hoped Charles would follow your lead, and you would guide him, but now he has already ruined his life, and you seem to be encouraging him! I am very disappointed."

Miss Bingley became more agitated and Darcy calmer.

"I thank you for speaking to my benefit, but I do not understand your disappointment, Miss Bingley, as I cannot understand how Charles has ruined his life. I know he will be happily married soon."

"Happily married into a family which is a shame to witness! How will he ever grow into society with such connections? And you, sir, you could not stand Mrs Bennet and her daughters, and now you seem to approve of all of them!"

"Caroline, please stop this conversation before you make a fool of yourself," Bingley attempted to temper his sister.

"I am a fool, Charles? What would you say about yourself and your sudden decision to marry a woman with no dowry, no connections, and not much personality either? Against all our expectations? She just smiles mindlessly, as Mr Darcy himself said last year!"

"Caroline! Mind your words, please! I shall not allow..."

"You cannot stop me from speaking my mind, Charles! Especially as it is the truth! Am I the only one capable of seeing the reality now? A reality, I might add, that Mr Darcy also noticed last November and agreed with me! Can you not understand that Eliza Bennet came to Pemberley on purpose? She said it was a coincidence, but undoubtedly it was all by design! She convinced you to return to Netherfield and to propose to her sister!"

"Caroline, this is ridiculous, truly," Bingley rolled his eyes. "And there is something I have to tell you—"

"There is nothing you can tell me that will change my mind, Charles. Last year, Mr Darcy agreed with me that Jane Bennet did not return your imprudent affection and only tried to attract you into a marriage advantageous for their family, surely pushed by her own mother! Surely you cannot deny you said so, Mr Darcy!"

Darcy sipped from his cup of coffee. His headache had slightly diminished, and he was in no mood to have it sharpened again by entering an argument with Caroline Bingley.

"Miss Bingley, I believe we already canvassed this matter at length at Pemberley. I shall not deny what I said, but that was a year ago when my knowledge was scant and my judgment faulty. It has been a long time since I have been convinced that Jane Bennet will make an excellent wife to Bingley and that Miss Elizabeth Bennet is one of the handsomest women of my acquaintance."

Miss Bingley was disconcerted by such a straight answer, but she kept her chin up and her glare sharp.

"I am surprised to hear such praise from you in regard to a woman you once took in derision, Mr Darcy."

"I am surprised you are surprised, Miss Bingley. If I recollect correctly, you were the first person to whom I confessed my admiration for Miss Elizabeth's fine eyes. Surely you remember that, too."

"Well, yes...I do, but I was sure it was only a joke. It should have been, and remained so. And you should be careful how you speak of Miss Eliza, her mother might believe you are courting her. That woman has no wit and no decency," Miss Bingley concluded with a victorious grin.

Darcy sipped more coffee.

"Yes, I remember you mocking me about having Mrs Bennet as a mother-in-law. It was last year, at Sir William Lucas's party. And you imparted more advice for my felicity upon marrying, here, at Netherfield, when Miss Bennet was recovering. You will be happy to know that I took your suggestion to heart, and I proposed to Miss Elizabeth. We are engaged to be married soon."

His calm voice and light countenance made the two sisters — and even Hurst — look at Darcy in stunned disbelief. To them, it sounded like an unfortunate joke meant to irritate them, although the moment was very ill chosen. Miss Bingley blinked repeatedly, glaring from him to her brother, trying to speak, but no words came out. Mrs Hurst forgot to breathe and choked, making Hurst rise to pat her back unceremoniously until she started to cough.

Finally, Miss Bingley managed to articulate, "Surely, you are not in earnest. It cannot be...this must be a poor joke...a pathetic joke...it is, is it not?"

"It is not a joke, Caroline," Bingley replied while Darcy remained impassive. "We shall marry the Miss Bennets in a month, in a double wedding. That is what I was trying to tell you before you made a fool of yourself. I suppose it is too late now."

Miss Bingley turned so red that her face seemed to boil, and she tried to stand up, but her knees refused to support her.

Unsteady, she tried to sit back down, but she almost missed the chair, which wobbled from the uneven weight, and her fingers did not find purchase on the edge of the table, so she had to struggle to regain a dignified posture. Bingley hurried to help her, but she rejected him angrily and stood up again, pushing the chair furiously aside, knocking it over. As she stormed out of the room, she noticed some servants staring from the doorway, attracted by the commotion, then disappearing into the hall in haste. She yelled at them and then at her sister, who was running after her.

"Well, if we have finished eating, I am going to Longbourn. Are you coming, Darcy?" Bingley asked.

"Of course. I look forward to it."

"May I join you?" Hurst asked. "There is nothing amusing in being at Netherfield now."

"Most certainly. Mr Bennet is an excellent host, and his brandy is good. I am sure he would welcome you," Bingley said.

"Good. Let me fetch my coat. So, Darcy, are you really engaged to Miss Elizabeth?"

"Of course I am, Hurst. I would not joke about such a serious matter."

"How interesting. By design or mere coincidence, Miss Elizabeth's arrival at Pemberley was very fortunate."

"More fortunate than you can imagine, Hurst," Darcy assured him as they all left the manor.

∞∞∞

"Lizzy, you have been awfully quiet all morning!" Mrs Bennet said as the family gathered for breakfast. "I imagine you must be upset that you will not receive a marriage proposal as good as Jane's. But it is your fault alone, miss. Mr Collins was a good enough catch, and you refused him. You could have been in Charlotte's place by now!"

"God forbid, Mama," Elizabeth said, rolling her eyes.

"So, Mrs Bennet, you would have been pleased if Lizzy had married Mr Collins?" Mr Bennet enquired in a tone that tried to conceal his amusement.

"Of course I would have! She could have been the future mistress of Longbourn and not allowed Charlotte Lucas to throw us out as soon as you die!"

"I shall try and overlook how indifferently you talk about my demise. I am sorry you suffered such disappointment though," her husband continued. "I wonder what Lizzy could say or do to compensate for it."

"Nothing, I assure you! Nothing at all! Thank God I love her, although she tries my nerves often, and I do not understand her most of the time!"

"Lizzy, it is true that you do try your mother's nerves often enough. You should try to repay her forbearance and generosity, really. Do you not have some news for her?"

"I do, but I had hoped we could finish breakfast in peace, Papa," Elizabeth replied, arching her eyebrow reproachfully.

"Well? What news? I warned you I could not care less about the Collinses' heir or about that Mr Wickham of yours! I was the only one who warned you that he might be a scoundrel, but you are such a headstrong girl, you never listen! How you went on about his misfortunes! I never liked him!"

"That is not true, Mama!" Lydia cried. "You always liked Mr Wickham and said he was the most handsome officer!"

"Oh hush, child, do not speak nonsense! Why would I have cared that he was so handsome and charming and um…so, Lizzy, what is it?"

Elizabeth turned her chair to her mother and pulled it a little closer, looking at Jane who sat opposite her and then at her father for support.

"Mama, there is something important I wish to tell you. Just try not to become too overwrought, you know it is bad for your nerves."

"You should have worried for my nerves when you refused Mr Collins, and now you will become a spinster! Luckily, your sister will marry Mr Bingley! He has five thousand a year! Five thousand! He will…but no matter now. So, what is it? Your news?"

"I do not know how to say this. Mama, you should not be concerned about me becoming a spinster or a burden on Mr Bingley at all. In fact, while I was in Derbyshire, Mr Darcy proposed, and I accepted."

She waited, but her words seemed to have no immediate effect.

"Proposed what, Lizzy? This game is rather annoying, you know."

"Proposed marriage, Mama. He asked me to marry him, and I accepted." Elizabeth smiled, but her mother frowned in confusion.

"Who proposed marriage to you?"

"Mama! Mr Darcy did, I just told you."

"Mr Darcy? This is a poor joke, Lizzy. You resemble your

father too much, and I shall not admit to being mocked by my own daughter!"

"I promise I am not mocking you. This is a wretched beginning, indeed. I depended on you to believe that a marriage proposal had been made to one of your daughters, Mama. Mr Darcy asked me to marry him. Uncle Gardiner was the first to give his consent, and yesterday he spoke to Papa too." Elizabeth's smile remained, while her mother's face looked like all the blood had drained from it.

"He did, I can testify to it," Mr Bennet confirmed.

"Mr Darcy proposed to you? This cannot be!" Lydia cried.

Mrs Bennet was still incredulous. "Mr Darcy proposed to you? But how? Why? He always disliked you. He did not even wish to dance with you!"

"He never disliked me, Mama. Quite the opposite. While it is true we have not always been on the best terms, we have put the past behind us. We are engaged, and if you approve of it, we shall marry in a month."

Mrs Bennet's face changed expressions with worrisome speed. She kept seeking a hint that her daughter and husband were joking at her expense, but there was none. She slowly replayed Elizabeth's every statement, word for word, fearing to admit its meaning.

"Mr Darcy proposed marriage to you, you said? And your uncle and aunt know that?"

"Yes, Mama."

"And he has already spoken to your father?"

"Yes, Mama. He will confirm it himself as soon as he arrives today."

"He will come here?"

"Of course. Is that not what Mr Bingley and other engaged men do? Visit their betrothed?" Elizabeth continued, amused that her mother's reaction had not been quite as she expected.

Lydia broke the stunned silence, crying, "But this cannot be! You cannot marry him, he is an arrogant, unpleasant, and cruel man, Wickham told me as much! You know what he did to poor Wickham! It is impossible! How could you?"

"Hush, child! You do not know what you are saying," Mrs Bennet scolded her favourite daughter so harshly that everyone startled. "Stop saying it is impossible!"

She stood up, then leant against the back of her chair, seeking support. Then she took a few steps from the table, and a few more, then came back, pacing the room until she finally stopped, facing her daughter.

"Are you sure Mr Darcy proposed marriage to you, Lizzy?"

"Of course I am, Mama. He came last night to speak to Papa directly, as you saw. We discussed marrying in a month."

"Marrying in a month? Are you sure?"

"Very much so, Mama. He will enquire after your opinion too, I suspect. Mama, I know his behaviour has been proud and arrogant in the past and you never liked him, but I assure you—"

"Never liked him? How can you say something so silly, Lizzy?" Mrs Bennet burst out again, this time with a force that could not be stopped and made her pace around the room again.

"How could anyone not like him? Such a tall, handsome man! Of course, he is proud and arrogant, he has every reason to be! I would be too, if I was in his place! A month? So soon? I have always admired him, to be sure! His uncle is an earl, is he not? And so was his grandfather!"

Mrs Bennet paused a moment to catch her breath before

resuming her monologue. "Ten thousand a year and probably more! And he proposed to my Lizzy? You will marry in a month? I am sure he will procure a special licence! He has to! Dear Lord — Mr Darcy! My dear Lizzy, how rich and important you will be! Let me kiss you! What a clever girl you are! I knew you could not be so clever for nothing! Mr Darcy! I cannot believe it!"

"So, my dear, may I presume you are no longer upset with Lizzy for refusing Mr Collins? Only minutes ago you seemed devastated," Mr Bennet jested.

"Mr Collins? Who cares about that tedious man? And by the way, you are to be blamed for Mr Collins, Mr Bennet! Why do you have such an annoying cousin? And why did you even invite him to Longbourn? The audacity of him to propose to Lizzy! God forbid she could have accepted him, and poor Mr Darcy would have suffered from jealousy! What a tragedy could have occurred, and it would have been your fault, Mr Bennet. Thank God Lizzy was so clever as to reject him!"

Mr Bennet was perplexed at such a twisting of the facts, and Elizabeth looked at him with mocking compassion. If Mrs Bennet stated it was his fault, nothing could contradict her.

Mrs Bennet continued to chatter and pace the room for a while. She stopped as she spotted through the window Mr Darcy himself, together with Mr Bingley and Mr Hurst. His appearance in person left Mrs Bennet silenced by emotions, and she pressed her hand over her chest, her heart pounding almost as strongly as Elizabeth's.

By the time the gentlemen entered, all the ladies were demurely and properly seated, and all eyes turned towards Darcy with apparent curiosity. However, it lasted only a moment before Mrs Bennet jumped to her feet and stepped forward with her hands outstretched towards Darcy.

"Mr Darcy, I was just told the most extraordinary news,

and I am deeply honoured to welcome you to my home! Please come in. Sit here, near Lizzy, and I shall sit over here. I cannot tell you how happy I am to see you here, sir. Would you stay for dinner tonight? If so, please tell me what your favourite dishes are! Mr Bingley has had his favourites cooked for two weeks now, and I noticed he eats anything, regardless."

Darcy touched her arm with a polite, gentle, but determined gesture which interrupted her.

"Mrs Bennet, I beg you not to trouble yourself in any way for me. I wish nothing in particular but the same lovely dinner as last night. I am delighted to be at Longbourn, in the company of your family. And, if you approved as Mr Bennet already did, I hope to be able to call it my family too in a month's time."

His tone, his familiar gesture, and the statement that dissipated all Mrs Bennet's remaining fears of a misunderstanding caused a new eruption.

"My dear Mr Darcy, be assured that you have my approval for anything you wish to do! Anything at all!" she exclaimed, causing Elizabeth a rush of deep mortification.

"I thank you for your trust, ma'am. This brings me to another favour I would kindly wish to ask you. In order to marry as soon as possible, we discussed having a double wedding with Bingley and Miss Bennet. Unless such an arrangement would displease you, of course. But we insisted on it so you may all come to spend Christmas at Pemberley."

Mrs Bennet's mouth remained wide open, as did her eyes; she tried to reply, but her mind was blurred. The double wedding meant she would only have one occasion to brag and boast about instead of two. But that also meant a quick arrangement so Darcy had no time to change his mind, as well as the added prospect of Christmas at Pemberley, which would surely make Lady Lucas and her other friends die of jealousy.

"My dear Mr Darcy, I would never deny you any favour you would do me the honour of asking. You can marry whenever you wish, sir. And so can you," she addressed the other three betrotheds with condescension and a sense of pride and self-importance like never before in her entire life.

Chapter 17

The weeks of engagement passed in haste and anticipation for the betrothed couples and with even more joy for Mrs Bennet, causing a commotion which affected Longbourn as well as half of Meryton. She was torn between expressing her admiration for her two sons-in-law but secretly favoured Darcy more, as she whispered to Elizabeth.

To his credit, Darcy bore all the attention reasonably well, and he slowly learnt to be more amused than irritated by Mrs Bennet's behaviour, as well as by Mr Bennet's constant teasing, which was equally uncomfortable. The long walks with Elizabeth, where they enjoyed intimate conversations, mutual expressions of love, and some delightful moments of privacy, the chance to sit by her side at the dinner table and sometimes take her hand without anyone noticing, the time spent in the library making plans with his future wife, and the daily countdown to the moment of the wedding made everything worth the while.

Mrs Bennet called on her sister and all her friends in Meryton to announce the happy event the very day she learnt about Elizabeth's engagement — news that was first received with scepticism and doubt. If Mr Bingley's proposal to Jane was an expected consequence of his long-witnessed admiration for the pretty young lady, the proud and arrogant Mr Darcy marrying Elizabeth Bennet, when their mutual dislike was equally universally known, seemed incomprehensible. And yet, after much disbelief, rumours, and wondering, it proved to be as real as Mr Darcy's obviously improved manners. Consequently, the Bennets' unexpected good luck became a subject of jealousy and gossip.

Against his will, Darcy was forced to travel to London twice during the period prior to his wedding, to settle some unexpected problems. The major one was caused by Wickham who — just as Darcy had feared — broke the arrangement and returned to London. Having a man who followed Wickham, Darcy had been immediately informed. Being thus taken from Elizabeth infuriated him exceedingly, and he showed no mercy and no patience for the man who had affected his life so often. Therefore, he applied to the judge with the settlements of the debts, and Wickham was confined and placed in debtors' prison. Marshalsea was a drastic step that Wickham did not expect and Darcy did not feel comfortable making. However, Colonel Fitzwilliam suggested it was better than *'just shooting that scoundrel'*, which was the second option. Darcy had no intention of leaving Wickham to rot in such a place, but if there were a situation appropriate to induce the man to reconsider his actions in haste, this was it.

The plan was to release Wickham as soon as another commission was found for him. The one in the North was no longer available to him, so Colonel Fitzwilliam recommended searching for other employment abroad, although the colonel found it ridiculous that Darcy bothered himself with anything related to Wickham only weeks prior to his wedding. Eventually, the colonel promised to make use of his connections and secure a place for him in one of the regiments leaving for the continent.

Equally disturbing was Lady Catherine de Bourgh, who received the news of Darcy's engagement with disbelief at first, then with ire and spite. She wrote Darcy several letters sent by express and some more to her brother demanding assistance from the earl. All the replies she received only angered her more and made her express her displeasure against Mr Collins and his wife until Charlotte decided it was the time to visit her family in Meryton.

His aunt's offensive and violent words against Elizabeth made Darcy cut all connection with Lady Catherine until he received proper apologies.

Once he returned to Netherfield, Darcy and Elizabeth were together most of the time, just like the other betrothed couple. They dined at Longbourn nearly every day; Mr Bingley did not host any parties at Netherfield as his sisters continued to show their disapproval for the upcoming weddings and, surprisingly, act with little civility even after Georgiana, the colonel, and his brother the viscount arrived to attend the wedding.

The sisters planned to return to London the same day of the wedding ceremony, a decision which nobody attempted to contradict. The invitation to Pemberley for Christmas was politely extended to them too but — much to Hurst's disappointment — they harshly declined it. Again, it was a decision nobody attempted to contradict either.

On a bright October morning, little more than one year after Netherfield had been let at last and Mr Bingley had brought his friend Mr Darcy with him, all Mrs Bennet's maternal wishes and hopes were fulfilled.

In Longbourn church, the two eldest Bennet sisters wedded the gentlemen of their dreams, in the presence of their neighbours, the Gardiners, and of course the distinguished guests from London, whose presence showed the support of Darcy's family. Braving the displeasure of Mr Darcy's illustrious aunt and the esteemed patroness of her husband, Charlotte Collins was there too, congratulating her friend Elizabeth Darcy and rejoicing in her good fortune.

It was universally admitted among those in attendance that Miss Elizabeth looked almost as beautiful as her sister Jane and Mr Bingley almost as handsome — although not so tall and rich — as his friend Mr Darcy.

Mrs Bennet's nerves proved to be strong enough to keep her relatively composed during the ceremony and afterwards at the wedding breakfast. The only reason for displeasure was that Mr and Mrs Darcy planned to leave for London immediately, so they could reach their home by nightfall. However, she did not argue, consoling herself with the upcoming meeting at Pemberley and the more immediate possibility of boasting, "Oh, they needed to depart so soon because Mr Darcy insisted on arriving at their *townhouse* as soon as possible, you see, impatient to introduce the servants to the new *Mrs Darcy.*" Besides, she had long promised to approve of anything Darcy wished to do, and she would not dream of breaking her word to him.

The Gardiners returned to London too, as the children had remained at home for the wedding. Also, Colonel Fitzwilliam and the viscount had urgent business to attend to, while the Bingley sisters were already long gone.

A warm farewell was shared, and even Mr Bennet shed a tear when his favourite daughter embraced him. With Darcy, he only exchanged a nod and a glance; everything had been said and cleared between them.

Finally, the carriages — Darcy's being so large and elegant, as Mrs Bennet repeated countless times — started to move, while the waving and shouted well wishes and goodbyes continued until it disappeared from sight.

Darcy's carriage was indeed too large for two people, but inside, the sudden silence following many days of bustle was most welcome.

The newly-married couple looked at each other, their smiles slightly awkward; for the first time since they had been pronounced man and wife, they were finally by themselves, but the long-desired intimacy made them uneasy.

"We should be in London by late afternoon. But it might get dark before we arrive," Darcy said.

"I am not worried about it getting dark. I am glad we shall be home today," she replied. "I am surprised that Georgiana preferred to travel with my uncle and aunt, though."

"You should not be surprised. My dear sister is wise beyond her years, and she assumed I would enjoy a private journey with my new wife. There is nothing I wanted more than to finally be alone with you. Am I distressing you with my enthusiasm?" he asked, as he noticed she was blushing.

"No, not at all. In truth, I am relieved that I am not the only one who is eager. I dearly love Georgiana, but I am glad I am alone with you," she admitted.

He took her hand and brought it to his lips, while his arm encircled her shoulders, pulling her closer.

"We shall have one stop on the road, already agreed upon with Mr Gardiner. My cousins will probably press on ahead, as they have another engagement tonight."

"It was very kind of the colonel and the viscount to attend the wedding, and I hope to see them again soon. But shall we stay long in town? I assume Georgiana will come with us to Pemberley and the rest of my family will join us later on, for Christmas."

"In fact, I spoke to Georgiana yesterday. She and Mrs

Annesley will travel together with your family, at the beginning of December."

"Really? But why?"

"Because I asked her to...I want to make this first journey home to Pemberley alone with you. We have already shared a long and distressing journey. Now, I would like to travel with you by my side, in my arms, with no hurry, no distress, and no worries."

"Oh..." she sighed, pleased, and settled more comfortably against his side. "That would be wonderful. I just hope Georgiana does not mind."

"Not at all. Besides, you will have time to visit and talk to her in the coming days. For the time being, she and Mrs Annesley will stay in her house."

"Will she?"

"Yes...I am a very selfish man, and I wish to share your company with nobody, at least for a few days."

"Then you might say I am a very selfish woman, too, as there is nothing I would like more."

"I am glad to hear that," he said, then his lips found hers, and there was silence in the carriage for a while.

"To answer your question," he continued whilst catching his breath and putting a bit of distance between them lest at the next stop he would not be able to stand in the Gardiners' presence, "the length of our stay in London is undecided yet. I would like to leave for Pemberley very soon, but I am afraid there are some issues that will require our presence for a month."

"The business with Wickham, I assume?"

"Yes, that would be one of them. I admit I do not wish to leave London without knowing he has gone one way or another.

It is difficult to find him a commission in another regiment, though. His reputation precedes him, and not in a good, worthy way. No officer in command wishes for the troubles that accompany him. My cousin asked for a relocation to one of the regiments going to the continent, but I know the risks and dangers would be greater than being a militia lieutenant, so I have not yet agreed."

"So, what will you do? Is it necessary to take so much trouble with him? Can you not just let him be?"

"I could. But I cannot leave him in prison, so I must decide either way. But enough of that scoundrel, I do not wish to waste our time speaking of him. It is just one of the tiresome issues that forces us to stay in London."

After as short a stop as necessary to refresh themselves and exchanging a few words with the Gardiners, declining the offer to join them for a light meal, they resumed their journey to London.

"I confess being more nervous about meeting your uncle and aunt. Although, if I were to judge from the colonel and the viscount, they cannot be too frightening," Elizabeth said.

"They are not. I am grateful to my aunt for hosting a dinner for us. Her support will be helpful in easing your first steps into the so-called first circle. Although, I confess I do not care much for it. Neither do my cousins."

"That is because you were born into it. To me, it is important to take the right steps, because it is not about Elizabeth Bennet, but about Mrs Darcy. I am not ignorant of my duties and responsibilities or my place in society."

He gently caressed her face and stole a brief kiss. "You are just as perfect as Mrs Darcy as you were as Elizabeth Bennet, my love."

"That is not much in terms of encouragement, as we both know I was far from perfection. In fact, I suspect you were tired of perfectly accomplished ladies, and my imperfections drew your attention."

"Your sparkling eyes drew my attention first. Then your smile and your sharp mind. But also," he continued, leaning further towards her until his lips tantalised her ear, "your enchanting figure captured my interest too. Especially when you walked with Miss Bingley around the room, do you remember? I do not know whether it was that *certain something* in your manner of walking, but I admit I slept very little and very ill that night."

She shivered from the sensation of his lips on her skin, although she was accustomed to it by now and it had caused her many sleepless nights too.

"I did not imagine that evening that my walking would have such an effect upon you, sir."

"How ridiculous I was to assume you understood my admiration, when you were busy despising me."

"No woman would easily forgive a man who called her tolerable and refused to dance with her, Mr Darcy."

"I do not expect to be easily forgiven, Mrs Darcy. Quite the opposite. I shall put in any effort to please you for years to come," he whispered, his lips tantalising her again.

"No effort is needed, sir, since I have long forgiven you," she answered, turning her head so her lips met his.

"I am sorry to hear that, Mrs Darcy! I have put some thinking into how to earn your forgiveness, and I think I have found just the way to persuade you. You must allow me..." After that, the conversation was scarce until the carriage stopped in front of Darcy's townhouse.

∞ ∞ ∞

The young maid withdrew discreetly, closing the door behind her; she was not needed any longer, but she had done her job more than satisfactorily.

Elizabeth stared at her image in the mirror, blushing slightly noticing how revealing the silk, creamy nightgown was. Mrs Gardiner had purchased it, and Elizabeth had been reluctant to wear it, although she admitted it looked and felt lovely on her.

Elizabeth was neither ignorant nor naïve, and she knew what to expect from that night; in fact, she was thrilled and eager to share and fulfil her love with her husband.

However, she also felt nervous, anxious, shyer in her gestures than her thoughts.

She touched her hair again, which was falling loose on her shoulders. It was slightly damp, as she had had a bath drawn in her room as soon as the introduction to the servants — their servants! — had been completed and dinner and the brief tour of the house was over, which occupied most of the evening.

Now, it was close to midnight, and she was waiting for her husband to join her.

"You are more beautiful than in the dreams that kept me awake so many nights, Mrs Darcy," she heard his voice and then his steps.

She turned, wearing a little smile, glancing at him. He was freshly shaved, with his hair also wet and curled on his temples, with the top buttons of his nightshirt opened. He was wearing loose trousers that revealed his ankles, and the sight of his bare skin increased her nervousness.

"Are you comfortable, my love? All is well, I hope?" he asked.

"Yes, all is perfect, indeed. Especially now that you are here," she replied.

He kissed both her hands and closed his arms around her.

"You are more beautiful than in my dreams," he repeated, "and I am happier than I ever imagined, my dearest, loveliest wife."

"So am I...happier than I imagined," she repeated. "But you should tell me more of those dreams one day, Mr Darcy," she teased him to cover her anxiety. "I have asked you several times, but you have refused to share them. Is it proper for a gentleman to keep secrets from his wife?"

He held her closer in his embrace, and her hands slipped around his waist and glided slowly up and down, feeling the heat of his body and the sinewy muscles of his back through the thin linen, while her face lifted to meet his adoring stare.

"I have kept the secret from my betrothed, as it was not something I would dare to share with Miss Elizabeth Bennet. However, I am ready to reveal all my dreams to Mrs Elizabeth Darcy, if she wishes to hear of them."

"She does...I do...very much so," she whispered, her lips trembling in anticipation of touching his.

"As I told you once, I would by no means suspend any pleasure of yours, Mrs Darcy. But instead of telling you, would you not allow me to show you?" he tempted her, an instant before his lips captured hers.

She had no time to voice her answer, but her acceptance was clearly expressed, beyond any doubt. And there was no time for dreaming that night, as they fell asleep very late, when the dawn broke the darkness. By that time, there were no secrets left unshared between them.

THE END

About Michelle

Drawing on her background in the drug industry and research, Michelle knows that the best cure for the mind is a good book and a healthy imagination.

Michelle discovered Jane Austen because of the Hollywood adaptation of Pride and Prejudice, with Lawrence Olivier, when she was fourteen. She has never looked for Mr Darcy because she thinks she has more similarities with him in character and perhaps more than she would like to admit with Lady Catherine too!

A greedy reader and a stingy sleeper, Michelle fell into the JAFF universe in early 2000 and happily witnessed some great stories coming to life. Steadfast cheerleader, prolific commenter and opinion-giver, sometimes headstrong and obstinate, especially when defending Darcy who, in her eyes, can do no wrong, she made a lot of friends among the authors and keeps in contact with a lot of them.

Encouragement from a dear friend, help from a magical red-penned one, and a sudden rise in courage persuaded her to finally put to paper some ideas that had been dancing in her mind for some time.

Michelle is the author of a very well received first book, "Happy by Accident... or Not?" and of the best seller "An Unpleasant Sort of Man".

"Undoubtedly by Design" is Michelle's third book.

Michelle would love to hear from you!
@: michelledarcy1967@gmail.com
Insta: pemberleymichelle
FB: Michelle d'Arcy

Books By This Author

Happy By Accident... Or Not?

"Happy by Accident...or Not?" is a Regency "Pride and Prejudice" novella variation that combines romance, humour, a little bit of angst, original twists and new characters mingling with the well-known and much-loved characters from the original novel.

The story begins the day after the party at Mrs. Phillips' house and the disturbing conversation during which Wickham reveals to Elizabeth his past misfortunes caused by Darcy.
On a cold autumn morning, Elizabeth takes a long walk to clear her thoughts and to escape Mr. Collins's annoying attentions.

Her solitary reverie is interrupted by cries for help and she discovers Mr. Bingley, who has fallen from his horse and is lying at the edge of a marsh. While Elizabeth tries to assist him, Darcy appears in search of his friend. With the threat of a storm approaching, Darcy hurries to fetch more help and Elizabeth remains with Bingley — a good opportunity for them to disagree about Darcy's character.

Mr. Bingley's wounds are not severe, but serious enough to affect his plans for the ball. Also, the disclosure of his argument with Miss Elizabeth will trouble Darcy, contradicting all his previous beliefs about the woman he secretly admires.
Therefore, the two gentlemen must decide how they want to proceed with the ladies of their hearts.

With several surprise visitors attending the Netherfield Ball, with opinions and feelings changed, with secrets unveiled and the truth finally exposed, our beloved couples will interact, argue, reconcile, bear some misunderstandings and suffer from a little bit of jealousy before they reach their well-deserved 'Happily Ever After'.

An Unpleasant Sort Of Man

A secret encounter at Oakham Mount, an unexpected and unknown witness, a fight that unearths dark revelations — all are instrumental in changing Elizabeth Bennet's beliefs, born from pride and tainted by prejudice, one cold November morning.

At Longbourn, the upcoming Netherfield ball is considered to be proof of Mr Bingley's admiration for Jane and is anticipated with much enthusiasm. Only the irritating presence of Mr Collins and his irksome attention ruin Elizabeth's disposition and induce her to take a walk that will change her life — as well as the lives of others.

At Netherfield, Fitzwilliam Darcy, haunted by his ardent admiration for a certain lady, plans to return to London immediately after the ball, together with Bingley's family, leaving their troubles and distress behind.

On the evening of the ball, Elizabeth's spirit is heavy with remorse, while doubts leave her undecided as to how she should proceed. As Darcy considers asking Elizabeth to stand up with him for a set — the first and last he believes he will ever dance with her — the ball is interrupted by news of a most disturbing incident which will affect the entire neighbourhood.

From that very moment, everyone's plans will be altered. Suspicions and rumours will shake the calm and complacency of the quiet and peaceful town of Meryton as well as a lot of first impressions. Events will quickly unfold, more secrets will be revealed, previous relationships will change while improbable friendships and most unanticipated alliances will form and grow.

Fitzwilliam Darcy and Samuel Bennet are as different as two gentlemen can be, in age, consequence, fortune, opinions on responsibilities and familial duty, even the notion of proper behaviour. However, they slowly discover some common interests in their love of books, good brandy, peaceful time spent in the library, meaningful conversation, and their strong — though undisclosed for one party — affection for a particular lady of their acquaintance. Will this unlikely companionship survive the events?

Forced by circumstances and guided by honour, loyalty, and courage, Elizabeth and Darcy will have to act together, thus discovering themselves and each other. Will their journey ruin or strengthen their alliance? Will their partnership end in just friendship or blossom into something else entirely?

'An Unpleasant Sort of Man' is a full length novel (around 380 pages in print!) assembling all the elements of a classic JAFF story: romance, moderate angst, tension, a bit of mystery, witty dialogues, a lot of interaction between our dear characters, slow relationship growth, and character development, all focused around the beloved story of Elizabeth and Darcy!

Printed in Great Britain
by Amazon